'Who is Belle

Perhaps he didn't
Belle's name—th
discover that she could not begin to imagine.
But she would be foolish to panic. She must
brazen this out. She must keep a tight grip on
herself. She rose from the bed and walked
stiffly to the bathroom, dived under the shower,
then briskly rubbed herself down with a towel.
She would cope with this new nightmare.
Somehow. And overcome it.

Dear Reader

Easter is upon us, and with it our thoughts turn to the meaning of Easter. For many, it's a time when Nature gives birth to all things, so what better way to begin a new season of love and romance than by reading some of the new authors whom we have recently introduced to our lists? Watch out for Helen Brooks, Jenny Cartwright, Liz Fielding, Sharon Kendrick and Catherine O'Connor—all of whom have books coming out this spring!

The Editor

Stephanie Howard was born and brought up in Dundee in Scotland, and educated at the London School of Economics. For ten years she worked as a journalist in London on a variety of women's magazines, among them *Woman's Own*, and was latterly editor of the now-defunct *Honey*. She has spent many years living and working abroad—in Italy, Malaysia, the Philippines and in the Middle East. Currently, she lives in Kent.

Recent titles by the same author:

UNCHAIN MY HEART
MIRACLES CAN HAPPEN
LOVE'S VENDETTA
DANGEROUS INHERITANCE

NO GOING BACK

BY

STEPHANIE HOWARD

MILLS & BOON LIMITED
ETON HOUSE   18-24 PARADISE ROAD
RICHMOND   SURREY   TW9 1SR

*First published in Great Britain 1993
by Mills & Boon Limited*

© Stephanie Howard 1993

*Australian copyright 1993
Philippine copyright 1993
This edition 1993*

ISBN 0 263 77975 0

*Set in Times Roman 11 on 12 pt.
01-9304-48663 C*

Made and printed in Great Britain

CHAPTER ONE

THE room into which she had just stepped was filled with summer sunshine, so intense that Laura paused and blinked for a moment, only just able to make out the figure who was standing with his back to her in the huge bay window.

She could see that he was tall and muscularly built, black-haired and dressed in light trousers and shirt, and that all of his attention appeared to be focused on the Mediterranean seascape, as blue as crushed sapphires, that stretched beyond the window as far as the horizon.

'I'm Laura Miskin. I believe you wanted to speak to me.'

Laura addressed the broad back, wondering if he had heard her enter, wishing she'd at least been told his name before being ushered somewhat hurriedly into the room—and wondering, too, what it was about the tall figure, silhouetted in the bright sunshine that poured through the window, that caused a shaft of foreboding to strike at her heart.

The man did not answer her immediately. Perhaps he hadn't heard her? Laura wondered. She took another step forward and cleared her throat, observing to herself that, in spite of his stillness, there was an aura of intense dynamic power about this man. His stillness was the coiled supple stillness of a cat.

And then, surprising her, he spoke.

'That is correct. I do indeed wish to speak to you.'

He still hadn't moved, and though he spoke the words softly there was something in his voice that caused Laura to catch her breath. It was crazy, but she could have sworn that she knew that deep, rich voice.

Impossible, she told herself, screwing her eyes against the sunlight. The voice she had thought she heard belonged to the past. A past that had been laid to rest long ago.

And then he spoke again, still with his back to her. 'It was good of you to come all this way at such short notice. I hope your journey was pleasant and without problems?'

It had been both. The flight from a cloudy London to a Naples basking in summer sunshine had been enjoyable and had gone as smoothly as clockwork—as indeed also had the ferry ride from Naples to her ultimate destination, the island of Alba.

But Laura found herself unable to give voice to this assurance. A nightmare suspicion was unfurling in her head. She stared at the tall figure, his voice echoing in her ears. Part of her felt so certain, yet surely it was not possible? Surely fate could not have dealt her so treacherous a card?

And then, very slowly, the man turned round to face her and in that instant the ground beneath her feet dropped away.

Black eyes looked into hers, eyes as cold as the sea in winter. The eyes of Falco Roth. All her worst fears were confirmed.

The wide lips smiled cynically. 'Welcome to my home.'

Laura could not answer him. She had lost the power of speech. Every muscle in her body had suddenly turned to stone.

Falco's gaze had never flickered. With a merciless smile he told her, 'You've gone quite pale. I'm sorry if I shocked you. I can see you had no idea as to the identity of your new employer.'

It was the note of amused, sadistic arrogance in his voice that pierced through the fog that had momentarily descended on her and instantly snapped Laura back to her senses. *Of course* she was shocked—just as, no doubt, he had intended! Knowing Falco, he'd been hoping that in addition to turning pale she would oblige him by falling in a faint to the floor!

She straightened her spine and smiled a caustic smile, as she proceeded to correct him on one essential detail.

'I'm afraid you appear to have misunderstood,' she informed him crisply. 'You are in no way, shape or form my employer. All you are is a prospective client.'

'A client. Yes, of course. You are absolutely right.' Falco paused to let his eyes drive through her like rapiers. 'But then, that was always a problem of mine... Understanding the nature of our relationship.'

His words had caused her heart to press tightly inside her. Laura understood perfectly what he was getting at. She knew precisely the sins of which Falco Roth believed her guilty. And she hated and despised him for believing such things.

'I had the same problem—understanding our relationship.' It was an effort to answer coolly, yet somehow she did. She even managed to add, her tone sharp and dismissive, 'What a pity we couldn't both have realised sooner what a total waste of time the whole thing was. That, fundamentally, our relationship wasn't worth understanding.'

'How well you sum it up. A total waste of time. Though for you in the end at least there were certain compensations.'

'Thank heavens for that.'

By a miracle her voice held steady, in spite of the renewed flare of emotion deep within her. There had been compensations. Incalculably precious. But these were unknown to him. They were not what he was referring to.

What he was referring to was something base and shameful, a sin of greed that sullied and blackened her character. But let him believe whatever he wished of her. It did not matter in the slightest. That he could believe it merely proved the type of man he was.

Laura forced a cold smile. 'However, that is not the point. What matters now, particularly in view of past misunderstandings, is that we get the current situation straight right from the start. And the current situation is that you're the client—*prospective* client,' she amended quickly. 'And I'm the decorator whose services you wish to hire.'

As she was speaking, Falco had stepped away from the window, and now that he was no longer caught in the sun's glare Laura could see him much more clearly.

She felt her heart contract as she looked into his face with its strong, sculpted lines, bright black eyes and sensuous mouth. Once upon a time she had adored that handsome face. With her eyes and with her lips she had poured her love upon it. That face had been the sun that lit up the whole world for her. And she had believed, because he had told her so, that he adored her in return.

A sense of bitterness swept through her, and a sense of her own folly. Three years ago she had been forced to face the cruel truth. What she had believed to be love had been a worthless empty lie.

Falco was watching her in turn, his eyes travelling over her, taking in her simple, elegant outfit—straight white skirt and olive short-sleeved blouse.

He said, 'You haven't changed much. Still as beautiful as ever.' His gaze flitted over her small heart-shaped face with its peaches and cream complexion, wide blue eyes and soft-lipped mouth. Then the dark eyes narrowed. 'But you've changed your hair. That's a pity. I liked it longer.'

'Did you? How unfortunate. I like it shorter.'

Defiantly, triumphantly, Laura tossed her bobbed head. The shearing of her mane of long blonde hair—that glorious golden mane that had cascaded halfway down her back and which Falco had so delighted to run his fingers through—had been a deliberate, symbolic act of liberation. Three years ago, after their final turbulent encounter, she had gone next day to her local hair salon and had the whole lot brutally lopped off. And as she'd watched it fall in silky hanks to the floor, she had vowed to scourge Falco from her heart for ever.

That hadn't proved easy. Indeed, the agony had almost killed her. But in the end, with guts and will-power, she had succeeded.

And yet, as she stood there, acutely conscious of his dark scrutiny, the memory of that old agony crushed against her senses. Just for an instant, as a thrust of pain drove through her, she almost feared a cry of anguish might escape from her lips.

She pushed the feeling from her. It was weak and melodramatic. And besides he was an unworthy cause of such anguish. The only emotion he merited was the non-emotion of indifference.

Laura looked into his face, into those eyes as hard as diamonds, and reached down into that icy corner of her heart that was reserved exclusively and evermore for him.

She said, 'But we're not here to discuss my hairdo, so perhaps you wouldn't mind telling me what it is we're here for?'

'But, my dear Laura, you already know what we're here for. We're here to discuss your commission. Your commission to decorate my house.'

'*Prospective* commission.' She bit the words back at him. 'And I am not your dear Laura, so I would rather you didn't call me that.'

'What would you prefer me to call you?' Falco smiled at her cynically. 'Miss Miskin? Surely we know each other a little too well for that?'

Laura had a flash of remembrance. The warm touch of his flesh. It was an effort to stop her cheeks from flaming. Yes, once, they had known each other very well indeed.

She checked her racing heart. 'Plain Laura would be sufficient. I see no need for false endearments.'

'In that case, I shall do my best to restrain myself.' Falco paused and regarded her for a moment. 'There has already been more than enough falseness between us.'

'That's what I would have thought.' Laura eyed him steadily. 'Yet it would appear that for you there can never be enough.'

'Meaning?'

'Meaning simply the method by which you brought me here. I think an accurate description would be "under false pretences".'

His gaze never flickered. He countered with mock innocence, 'And what is that supposed to mean?'

'It means that if I had known that this house belonged to you, I would not, even for one moment, have considered the commission. I most certainly would not have come all the way here to Italy, and you could have saved yourself the price of my plane fare and expenses. For, needless to say, I'm turning down the commission.'

'You can't do that. You've already accepted it. You and I, my dear Laura, already have an agreement.'

'Not any more. Consider it cancelled.' She was tempted to add the false endearment 'my dear Falco'—his mocking repetition of 'my dear Laura' had not escaped her—but, when it came to it, the words stuck in her throat. Once, not so long ago, these words had had real meaning. He had been dearer to her at one time than the very air she breathed. And, even now, she could not bring herself to make a mockery of that ancient folly.

'I'm afraid you're going to have to look else-where for a decorator,' she told him.

'How very unprofessional of you.'

'Unprofessional? That's a joke! If anyone's un-professional, I would say that it's you! You con-cealed from me an essential piece of information. To put it bluntly, you tricked me into coming here!'

Her angry tone hid a sudden wave of panic. Why had he brought her here? Why had he tricked her? Was it possible—her worst nightmare—that he had uncovered her secret?

She frowned into his face, searching in vain for an answer, as she added, 'But there's one thing I can assure you of: there's no way you can trick me into staying!'

Falco said nothing for a moment, then amusement touched his eyes. 'Why don't you take a seat? Make yourself comfortable? I take it you will at least be staying long enough to have a drink?'

Laura smiled without humour at this small joke at her expense. He was good at jokes. He always had been. Hadn't their past relationship been one big joke—a joke he'd kept to himself until the final punchline?

But in response she simply said, 'Yes, I'll stay for a drink. I'd say a drink is the very least you owe me.' Then, looking a great deal more com-posed than she felt, she seated herself in a nearby armchair. 'I'd like a glass of fresh orange juice, if that's not too much trouble.'

'No trouble at all.' Falco stepped to the side-board and pressed the bell in the wall above it. 'Anna, my housekeeper, will be here in a moment to take your order.'

Laura almost laughed. 'I might have known there would be servants! You were always so good at getting others to look after you.'

'They don't do it for nothing. They're generously paid.' He held her eyes and for a moment the humour left his face. 'If anyone should know that you can get people to do anything if you pay them enough money, you certainly should.'

Laura felt her fists clench at that reference to the past. But, though the accusation stung, she made no effort to deny it. Instead, she answered defiantly, 'That's the way the world is. Few things are worth as much as money in one's pocket.'

Falco's dark brows drew together as he remained standing by the sideboard. He subjected her to a long, dissecting look. 'And that was quite a pocketful you walked off with. You certainly got your pound of flesh.'

'I'm a hard bargainer. And I knew your father could afford it. I also knew he was desperate to pay me off at any price.'

'I suppose that's some consolation.' Falco smiled a wry smile. 'At least no one can say you betrayed me for peanuts.'

Laura was grateful that at that moment the housekeeper appeared and she was spared the further scrutiny of that merciless black gaze. All at once her heart was jumping uncomfortably inside her. She could feel her breath rough and ragged in her throat.

That was all that really mattered to him. It helped salvage his pride to believe that at least it had taken a small fortune to induce her to walk out on him and their relationship three years ago. For his pride was the only part of him that had suffered. Certainly her betrayal had not damaged his heart.

She watched him as he spoke in Italian to Anna, a small, dark-haired woman with a round smiling face.

He, too, had changed little over the past three years. The dark hair was perhaps a little shorter, the lines of his face more firmly set, but he still exuded that air of total self-assurance that had once, in the early days, impressed and delighted her, until she had learned that it sprang from a ruthless lack of caring for anyone other than Falco Roth.

But as Anna departed, Laura pushed these thoughts from her and observed conversationally, her tone mildly complimentary, 'It sounds as though you've mastered the language.'

The remark had been intended less as a compliment than as a desperate bid to change the direction of the conversation. That brief, bitter exchange about the past she had found both deeply painful and acutely threatening. Who knew where discussions about the past might lead?

Falco, she sensed, had understood her strategy. And as he looked at her, she suspected he was about to block her attempt to shift their dialogue on to more neutral ground.

But he did not. Instead, he observed with a smile, 'I wouldn't exactly say I've mastered it. But I intend to. It's a very beautiful language.'

Laura relaxed just a little. 'Have you been learning it for long?'

'On and off for a couple of years now. I've had a number of Italian holidays that I enjoyed so much I decided it was time I bought a base here.'

'Quite an impressive base.' Laura glanced quickly round her. The villa was beautiful, though in need of redecoration.

'I bought it as it stood, with all the contents—most of which I intend to dispose of. No doubt my tenants will find a use for them.'

'Your tenants?' Her eyebrows lifted. 'You have tenants living in the house?'

'Not in the house. Scattered about the island. You see, I didn't just buy the house, I bought the entire island.' Falco at least had the grace to smile as he said it. 'There are about fifty or so inhabitants here on the island besides myself.'

Laura's eyebrows remained lifted. 'My,' she observed, 'the plumbing equipment industry must be doing well.'

That sharp-edged reference to his father's Midlands-based company, the source of all the considerable Roth wealth, Falco pointedly allowed to pass without comment. His gaze shuttered, he seated himself in the armchair opposite her and observed, as though they had never digressed from the subject, 'Italian is not a difficult language. During your stay here, you will no doubt pick up a fair smattering yourself.'

'*If* I were staying here, no doubt I would.' Laura smiled a cold smile. 'But, as I told you, I'm not staying.'

'And as I told you, we have an agreement.'

'An agreement you drew me into under false pretences and which I have not the slightest intention of honouring.' Laura sat back in her seat and narrowed her eyes at him, carefully camouflaging the spurt of panic within her, as again she wondered if he knew about her secret.

'What beats me,' she put to him, 'is why you would want *me* to do your house for you—and why on earth you'd go to the trouble of tricking me into coming here.' Inwardly, she steeled herself for his answer.

'Who said I tricked you into coming here?' Falco leaned back in his chair, his hair very dark against the pale blue damask upholstery, and hooked one leg at the ankle over the opposite knee. 'Who said it was I who chose you to do the house?'

'No one.' In her anxiety, she had simply assumed it. And the possibility that she might be wrong was deeply heartening. Yet Laura's tone was sceptical as she put to him, 'So, are you trying to tell me it was your girlfriend who chose me? I believe in co-incidence, but surely that's pushing it a bit?'

'Why? I understand you're considered to be in the top rank of London designers these days. Anyone arriving in London with the mission of finding a decorator would have a pretty good chance of choosing you.'

She wanted to believe him, more than anything, but that sounded a little too much like flattery to be convincing. 'I suppose it's possible, but it's still quite a coincidence.'

'Coincidences happen. Life is full of coinci-dences.' The dark eyes narrowed. 'And, as you said yourself, for what possible reason would I deliber-ately have chosen you?'

Laura's heart kicked inside her. Was that an honest denial or a quiet warning that he did indeed have a reason? And that that reason was the very one she feared.

She took a deep breath and fought to steady her nerves. She must assume the former and act accordingly, or there was the danger that out of panic she might end up betraying herself.

'OK,' she agreed, 'let's assume it was a coincidence. You sent your girlfriend over to London to find you a decorator and she came up with me.' She leaned forward in her seat and looked him in the eye. 'So why, when she told you who she'd picked, didn't you just tell her to go back and pick someone else? Surely her selection couldn't have thrilled you any more than it thrills me?'

'Perhaps I wasn't available when the arrangements were made? Perhaps by the time I knew, you were already on your way?'

Laura frowned. There was a remote possibility that was true. After all, the arrangements had been made very quickly. From her first meeting with the delectable flame-haired Janine Curtis to the drawing up of the agreement less than twenty-four hours had elapsed. And she had been heading for Alba two days later to spend two weeks getting to know the villa, an arrangement that Janine had insisted on most firmly.

Laura felt the tension inside her slacken, yet still a niggling doubt remained. 'How come Janine never once mentioned your name? From the way she spoke, I believed the villa was hers.'

Falco smiled a fond smile. 'I'm sure she intended no deception. But you know how girlfriends are. She probably thinks of it as hers.'

That was possible, too. Laura sat back and looked across at him, and through her own confused thoughts she was suddenly aware of an unexpected dart of sympathy for the girl. Once, in her innocence, Laura too had believed that her future and Falco's were destined to flow together. She wished Janine Curtis all the luck in the world. With a man like Falco she was going to need it.

Still she persisted, 'Even when I got here, she still didn't mention you. Not by name. She referred to you as the owner, told me you wanted to speak to me and more or less pushed me into the room.'

'That was most remiss of her. I apologise on her behalf. But you mustn't be too hard on her. She's just an ordinary girl.'

That thought had struck Laura. Though expensively coiffed and clothed, Janine Curtis was an unsophisticated sort of girl. In her mid-twenties, of an age with Laura, she was perfectly stunning in a slightly showy way, the sort of girl many men would be happy to be seen with. But though Laura had found her likeable, she had been sharply aware of the girl's lack of self-confidence, her air of insecurity, and of the almost total absence in her of what one might call social polish.

She smiled wryly to herself. Look who was talking! Once, she had been as lacking in social polish as Janine! She too had started out as just an ordinary girl. Any sophistication she had acquired had rubbed off on her gradually, thanks in the early days to her association with Falco and later to the privileged circles into which her profession had drawn her.

Janine, too, would learn. Falco would teach her. He was the sort of man who liked his women with a bit of polish.

At that thought an odd sensation gripped her. In the old days, Pygmalion-like, he had been her Professor Higgins. He had had so much to teach her and she had been so eager to learn. It hadn't occurred to her until it was too late that she was merely an amusement.

The door opened at that moment and Anna came in, carrying on a tray a huge jug of orange juice, two tall glasses and a dish of delicious-looking teacakes.

She laid the tray on a coffee-table between their two armchairs, filled the two glasses to the brim with orange juice and beamed in response to Falco's appreciative, '*Grazie*!'

'*Prego*,' she murmured—don't mention it—and left.

A thought struck Laura as she reached for her orange juice and took a cool delicious mouthful. 'Where is Janine? Why isn't she joining us? Surely she ought to be in on our discussion? After all, it would appear that she's responsible for my being here.'

'I expect she's gone swimming. She does most days around tea-time.' Falco helped himself to a cake and pushed the plate towards Laura. 'Do help yourself. They're quite delicious.'

'I hope you'll tell Janine I'm terribly sorry that after all the trouble she went to you've ended up without a decorator.' Laura helped herself to a tiny chocolate *bignè* and popped it in her mouth. He was right. It was delicious.

'So you really are serious about not staying?'

'Absolutely serious.'

'That's a pity.'

'Perhaps, but only a temporary inconvenience. Janine will soon find someone else.'

Laura was aware, as she spoke, of a rushing sense of relief. He was letting her off the hook, and that could mean only one thing—that this unfortunate encounter had indeed been a coincidence, that he was not, after all, aware of her secret, that he had not brought her here because of that.

She added in a buoyant tone, 'There are plenty of good decorators around.'

'I'm sure there are.' He was watching her closely. 'And I wonder what their opinion will be of you when I tell them how you reneged on our contract?'

Laura stared, dumb-mouthed, at him. Then she spoke. 'That isn't fair. If I reneged, it was for a good reason. Considering the nature of our past relationship—and how deeply we dislike each other,' she added for good measure, 'it would have been ludicrous for us to go ahead.'

It was as though she had not spoken. He took a mouthful of his drink, helped himself to another cake and chewed on it thoughtfully. 'I can probably, with a bit of juggling, fit in a trip to London next week. I won't send Janine. This time I'll go myself.'

He skewered her with a look. 'And to make up for this inconvenience, I shall take pleasure in apprising your colleagues in the trade of your utter and lamentable lack of professionalism.' He smiled. 'I'll be very surprised indeed if any of them shares your old-fashioned view that our past personal relationship is a valid excuse. After all, that ended a long time ago.'

Laura looked into his face. 'You wouldn't do that?' Suddenly, her heart was thudding inside her.

He smiled back at her flintily. 'Oh, yes, I would. You inconvenience me and I'll inconvenience you.' He observed her stricken face. 'You wouldn't like that, would you?'

Laura shook her head soundlessly. He had no idea what he was saying. He had no idea of the storm of fear he had awakened in her heart. For his threat to discuss her lack of professionalism with her colleagues was not what caused her now to gaze at him, blank-eyed with horror.

The fear that suddenly gripped her was far more terrible than that. For if he were to start discussing her with the members of her professional circle in London, sooner or later he was bound to discover the secret that she had vowed he must never know.

She lowered her eyes momentarily. She had no choice. Then she looked up at him, her cheeks ashen, and spoke through bloodless lips.

'OK, you win. I'll stay on and do the job.'

CHAPTER TWO

THERE followed a short silence as Falco sat watching her. Then he leaned back in his seat. 'A sensible decision. This way neither of us is inconvenienced. I'm glad you finally decided to see sense.'

Laura did not answer him. She felt stiff with emotion. She had escaped from the jaws of a potential bonfire only to find herself up to her neck in quicksand. How on earth would she survive this enforced collaboration with Falco? Just the thought of it made her blood run cold.

Those dark probing eyes of his had never left her face. He observed with false innocence, 'Quite frankly, it beats me why you bothered to make such a fuss in the first place. What harm can there possibly be in my hiring you to decorate my house?'

Laura breathed deeply to calm herself. 'No harm,' she replied tightly. 'I just consider it a little inappropriate in the circumstances. Perhaps smacking just a tiny bit of bad taste.'

'Bad taste? I can't see why.' He was enjoying her discomfort. 'After all, we are, and have been for a long time, two quite separate, independent individuals. And our current association is, of course, strictly professional.'

There was nothing surer than that! Laura cast him a cool look. 'Personally, I would have preferred to have no further associations with you of any nature whatsoever.' Then, in a tone laced with far more emotion than she'd intended, she blurted out, 'Quite frankly, I would have preferred never to have set eyes on you again!'

'Why, what's the problem?'

'There's no problem.'

'Can't you handle it?'

'Of course I can handle it.' But she flushed as she said it. Her heart all at once was a painful tangle of raw emotions. She forced herself to look at him. 'I can handle it,' she repeated.

For what seemed like a long time Falco continued to look at her, an amused, sceptical smile playing round his lips. It was not necessary for him to say that he did not believe her.

Then he observed, 'I just hope I can rely on your word. It's no use to me if you keep changing your mind.'

'I won't change my mind. I said I'll do it. I don't go back on my word once I've made a firm commitment.'

Falco smiled then, a dismissive, crushing smile. 'I take it you're referring to matters professional? In the personal sphere, as we both know, you tend to be rather less fastidious.'

Laura had half expected that shot across her bows, but she was unable to control the twist of pain it inflicted. His accusation was unjust, yet he was determined to go on believing it. It suited him to believe it. That had always been evident.

She drew a calming breath. So, let him believe it. What he chose to believe about her quite frankly couldn't matter less.

In a composed tone she answered him, 'Yes, I was speaking professionally. As you were at pains to assure me just a moment ago, matters of a professional nature are all that exist between us.'

'Quite so.' Harsh-eyed, he regarded her for a moment. 'Let's hope that in such matters you prove to be a little more honourable than you have demonstrated yourself to be in other areas of your life.'

Then he glanced at his watch and rose to his feet abruptly. 'I have things to attend to. Forgive me if I leave you to finish your orange juice alone. I'll ask Anna to show you to your room when you're ready.'

And with that he turned sharply on his heel and left the room.

More than four hours had passed since that hostile exchange, yet the words that had passed between them were still ringing in Laura's head as, upstairs in her room, she prepared for dinner.

'We dine at nine,' Janine had come to her room to inform her. 'Nothing formal. But Falco likes us to be punctual.'

It was a little after eight now, and Laura had just showered and washed her hair. She sank down in her bathrobe before the dressing-table, leaned forward and regarded her reflection in the mirror.

How had she got into this abominable situation? What on earth had she done to deserve such a fate? And how would she manage to come through it, she wondered, without cracking up and going crazy in the process?

She sighed. I've survived worse, she told herself sternly. And I'll survive this, too, even if it kills me!

Her fists clenched as she thought of the reason that had forced her to accept this odious arrangement. She had so much to protect. All that was most precious in the world to her. This arrangement with Falco was a small sacrifice to make if it ensured that her secret was kept safely from him.

She smiled a wry smile. Falco believed he had trapped her with his threat to slander her professional good name. So, let him believe it. He understood nothing. He even seemed to be labouring under the misapprehension that her reluctance to work for him was an indication that he still had some kind of emotional hold over her.

He believed she had a problem, that she couldn't handle it, that she'd be unable to cope with the enforced proximity that working for him would necessarily entail. Without the need for words his taunting eyes had told her that he believed she might still be carrying a torch for him.

How utterly ridiculous! Laura snapped to her feet impatiently. How dared he suggest such a ludicrous thing?

But even as she dismissed the notion angrily, she was aware of a surge of emotion within her, unexpectedly intense, pain and bitterness mingled. They were the very same emotions she had felt this afternoon when he had turned round to face her across the sunlit drawing-room.

Laura closed her eyes and breathed deeply for a moment. They were not the emotions she had expected to feel should she ever have the misfortune to run into him again. What she had expected to feel, what she had *hoped* she would feel, was not pain and bitterness, but cold indifference. And at the crucial moment it had not been there.

What did you expect? She turned on herself impatiently, blue eyes flashing at her reflection in the mirror. She had been caught off guard. She had felt plunged into the past. What she had felt this afternoon had quite simply been an echo of the emotions that had possessed her at their last meeting. Pain more fierce than she could endure and a sense of bitterness that had choked her.

But these were throwback emotions. In reality they meant nothing. What was real was the pool of cold indifference that she had nurtured in her heart over the past three years.

She frowned and made a solemn promise to herself. By the time she was through with this commission Falco would be as sure as she was of her indifference.

With a sigh Laura sank down once more on to the chair and regarded her reflection a little more kindly. That she no longer cared for him was beyond disputing, but it was unfair of her to castigate herself for having loved him once. The love she had felt for him had been pure and good and true. The love of innocence. The trusting love of youth . . .

It had been just under four years ago that she and Falco had first met, quite by accident, as tended to be the case with the events that shaped our lives the most.

Laura was twenty-one years old and a junior secretary at the Solihull-based Roth Engineering plant, where her father, an electrician, had worked for twenty-five years. Falco, five years her senior, was the boss's only son and at that time had been in charge of the sales department. All the girls at the plant had their eyes on Falco Roth.

All except Laura, by an odd quirk of fate. She had noticed him, of course. Falco Roth, all his life, was destined to be the type of man that women noticed. And she had admired him. He was handsome, charming, dynamic. But it had never crossed her mind, like some of the other girls, to pursue him. Pursuing men was definitely not Laura's style, and besides she'd had other ambitions on her mind.

At least that was how it had been until that fateful day when she had walked through a swing door and collided straight into him.

'I beg your pardon. My fault entirely.' He was smiling as he bent to help her gather up the papers she'd been carrying and that now were scattered about the corridor floor. 'I ought to be more careful where I'm going.'

'It was as much my fault as yours.' Laura was down on her knees, hurriedly snatching up the scattered documents. 'I wasn't paying attention. I was miles away.'

'Really? Then we suffer from the same affliction. Being mentally miles away from where I actually am is a condition I suffer from all the time.'

That was when, for the first time, Laura glanced up to meet his eyes, and she would remember forever the sensation that had hit her. It was as though a fist suddenly connected with her midriff. The breath left her body. For a moment she was speechless.

'Are you all right?' Those mesmeric bright black eyes, the like of which Laura had never before looked into, widened a little in concern. 'I didn't hurt you, did I, when I crashed into you like that?'

'No, no. Of course not.' Laura snatched her gaze away. 'I'm fine. Perfectly fine.' Her heart was beating strangely. She rose to her feet shakily. 'Thank you,' she told him, as he held out to her with a smile the piles of papers he had gathered. Then, as though her feet were on fire, she was hurrying off down the corridor.

For the rest of the day the thought of him haunted her. And in spite of her efforts it proved quite beyond her power to drive from her mind the image of those dark eyes and the wonderful way that they had smiled at her. And every time she thought of them her stomach twisted into knots.

That was why—in an effort to drive out such foolishness—Laura decided to miss the bus and walk home that evening. A three-mile hike would be most therapeutic. It would give her a chance to get her head straight.

It was just her misfortune that she had barely set out when the heavens suddenly opened and down came the rain.

'Come on. Hop in. Let me give you a lift.'

As a voice spoke, Laura whirled round and found herself looking into those same mesmeric black eyes she'd been struggling to forget. Falco had pushed open the passenger door of his little silver sports car and was leaning across the seat towards her.

'Come on. What are you waiting for? You're soaked to the skin.'

Her stomach was in knots again, her heart racing like a steam train. She felt shaky and peculiar. She forced herself to say, 'I don't need a lift, thanks. I'd really rather walk.'

'You'll do nothing of the sort!' Mock-ferociously, then, he scowled at her. 'Get in this instant or I'll get out and throw you in!'

In spite of his smile, Laura sensed he meant it. And besides, why argue? The honest truth was that more than anything in the world she wanted to accept his invitation.

So she climbed in, struggling to control her shaking limbs. 'This is really very good of you,' she said, winding up the window, clutching at her bag, not daring to look at him. 'I hope it's not too much out of your way, but I live on the other side of North Street.'

'It's not out of my way at all.' Falco slipped the car into gear, pressed the accelerator hard and shot away from the kerb. Then he smiled across at her. 'So, what on earth possessed you to go walking in the rain without an umbrella?'

Laura shrugged, feeling awkward. 'It wasn't raining when I started out. How was I supposed to know it was suddenly going to pour down?'

'A quick glance at the sky might have given you some hint.' He was teasing her. 'I suppose you didn't think of that?'

'As a matter of fact I didn't.'

'Miles away as usual?'

'Something like that.' If only he knew! She felt a guilty blush creep over her neck. Then, as they went whizzing past a junction, she spun round to inform him, 'I think you're miles away as well! You're going the wrong way!'

'Am I? That's good. It means our journey'll take longer.' He turned to meet her eyes, sending goose-bumps all over her. 'In fact, I know a route that'll take half an hour, at least.' He paused. 'Unless, of course, you're in a hurry?'

Laura was uncertain. 'No, not really, but——'

'But nothing.' He winked across at her, dark eyes dancing. 'Don't worry, Laura Miskin, I'm not about to kidnap you. All I want is a chance for us to have a chat.'

So, he knew her name. Her heart flared with foolish pleasure. He must have found that out this afternoon, after their collision in the corridor.

He glanced across at her again. 'Are you agreeable?'

'To our having a chat? Yes, I suppose so.' Her pulse was racing with silly excitement. 'What in particular do you want to chat about?'

'You, Laura Miskin. I want you to tell me all about you—and all about those secret daydreams of yours that cause you to go colliding into people through swing doors and setting off in thunder-storms without an umbrella.'

As she glanced away, filled with sudden con-fusion, he reached across and softly, fleetingly, touched her arm, causing her skin to jump and her heart to stand still. 'But you can start with the easy stuff. Like where you come from, where you went to school, how many brothers and sisters you have, how long you've been working for my father...and will you agree to have dinner with me tomorrow evening?'

Laura laughed, feeling the tension inside her melt away. His easy, light-hearted manner was catching. 'Which one do you want me to answer first?' she demanded, joking.

'The last one, of course.'

Again he met her eyes, and Laura felt a thrust of wild happiness rush through her.

'OK,' she said, sealing her fate. 'You're on!'

That was how the love-affair had started, the first and only love-affair of Laura's life. And she had known even then, as he drove her home through the rain, that this was the start of something special.

Their love had blossomed fast, yet at a pace that felt quite natural. For they were never like strangers. Not even in the beginning. Something had seemed to click instantly between them.

They understood each other. It was instinctive. Effortless. Ordained, Laura had told herself dreamily, in heaven.

And Laura had shared with him the secret dreams she'd shared with no one else. And he'd understood and encouraged her, just as she'd known he would.

'One day it'll happen,' he'd told her often. 'One day you'll be a top-class decorator. You have the eye. It's in you. I'm absolutely sure it is.'

'Do you really think so?'

'I don't just think it. I know it.'

And he'd done far more than simply encourage her with words. On her birthday, just a couple of months into their relationship, he'd presented her with the most wonderful birthday gift imaginable—a top-class correspondence course in interior decorating, something she'd dreamed of but known she could never afford.

Then there had been the trips to the auction rooms in London—art collecting, she had discovered, was a secret passion of Falco's—where she'd gained a wealth of knowledge about all sorts of things, from furniture to porcelain, from old masters to Victoriana. Doors she'd scarcely dared to knock on were suddenly flung open.

But all of that had been a small part of the magic between them. What had awakened Laura's heart was the wonderful love they'd shared.

She would remember forever the first time they had kissed. How the whole world had seemed to tilt on its axis as Falco had leaned towards her, his arms around her waist, his eyes burning into hers, and she, holding her breath, had raised her lips to his. Just to think of it, even years later, could make her scalp tingle.

And then there had been the first time they had ever made love.

By then they had become inseparable and both of them had known that sooner or later it was bound to happen. But, though she'd longed for it, Laura had known also that it was a gigantic step to take. Falco would be her first. It was not a boundary to cross lightly.

In the event, it had been the most beautiful experience of her life.

They had been at Falco's flat. He had cooked them both dinner. Cooking, Laura had discovered, was just another of his many accomplishments. And they had been lying together on the sofa, arms wrapped warmly around one another, chatting, laughing, exchanging kisses.

Then Laura had glanced at the clock. 'I'd better go,' she'd murmured.

Her tone had been reluctant, for the last thing she'd really wanted was to go home to the chilly bedsit she shared with a friend. These days, each time that she and Falco parted it almost felt like losing a limb. And he felt the same. That was what he had told her.

He'd tilted her chin and kissed her mouth softly. 'Stay the night,' he'd pleaded. 'Don't go, Laura.'

Laura had held her breath. Dared she? she'd wondered. For she'd known what would happen if she were to stay.

Falco had instantly understood her hesitation. He'd kissed her again. 'I want you,' he'd told her. 'I want you more than I can say. But believe me, sweet Laura, I wouldn't even be suggesting this if I wasn't already very sure of one thing...'

He'd stroked her cheek and held her eyes a moment, with a look that had caused her heart to judder. 'I wouldn't even think of making love to you,' he'd told her, 'if I weren't already sure you're the girl I want to marry.'

Laura's heart had stopped with happiness inside her.

'I love you,' he'd continued, a smile lighting his eyes at her utterly speechless, round-eyed expression. 'You don't have to say yes or no right now. But it's important to me that you should know how I feel.'

Laura had not given him her answer that unforgettable evening, though not because she was unsure

of what her answer should be. Rather because she
could not fully take in the enormity of what he'd
just told her. She had dreamed of such a thing,
many, many times, but had never dared to imagine
that it might actually happen.

Still, she'd managed to tell him, 'I love you, too.
And I'll stay. I want to. Very much.'

It was a decision she'd never regretted making.
Whatever had happened later, nothing could spoil
the memory of that wonderful, rapturous first night
together.

Like some knight bearing his damsel off to his
castle, Falco had whisked her from the sofa and
carried her through to the bedroom, instantly dis-
solving all her tension and turning it into raw excitement. For she had known then for sure what
she had already imagined, that making love with
Falco would be a multi-faceted experience—
thrilling, breathtaking, sensuous, and fun.

It had been all of these things, and much more
besides. The awakening of a side of her that had
been half dormant until then. The discovery and
exploration of a whole new set of senses. The
fulfilment and deepening of the wonderful love they
had shared.

For Laura had known, as she lay naked with him
that night, her flesh trembling with almost unbearable pleasure at the touch of him, that this new
intimacy had brought them even closer together.
She had felt bound to him forever as though with
hoops of steel.

Two months later, at Christmas, they had become
engaged. Much too quickly, some friends had told
her. Far too hastily, according to her mother. And

their critics had been right. For that had been the beginning of the end.

Laura had learned to appreciate that the romance would have ended anyway. Falco was not the committed fiancé that he had pretended to be. But the inevitable disintegration had been speeded up by his father.

Oscar Roth was a man universally known for his ruthlessness. And Oscar, unfortunately, did not approve of Laura. He had summoned her to his office one day and told her,

'I think you ought to know that I have no intention of ever allowing you to marry my son. I intend that Falco should do much better for himself than end up with some penniless little secretary who has nothing better to offer than some airy-fairy notions to spend her time decorating other people's houses.'

Falco had been angry when she'd told him what had happened.

'Pay no attention to what my father says,' he'd told her. 'The days when my father could tell me how to run my life ended a very long time ago.'

Laura had accepted that and demanded no more reassurances. Falco, she knew, was strong-willed and very much his own man—though she'd never entirely managed to understand the complex relationship he seemed to have with his father.

It had seemed an edgy relationship, often full of conflict, yet held together by some deep bond. She knew that Falco and Oscar often quarrelled, yet she knew also that Falco could be intensely loyal to his father.

Later, of course, she had understood perfectly the nature of the bond that held them together. They were birds of a feather. It was as simple as that.

But three years ago she had still been an innocent. Three years ago, when, for a second time, while Falco was away on business in Brussels, Oscar Roth had called her to his office, this time to offer her money to break off her engagement, then, when that had failed, to issue threats, threats that had left her no choice but to give in, even then Laura had believed that in the end he would not win, that nothing could stop her and Falco being together.

She had clung to that belief as she carried out Oscar's orders. Within twenty-four hours she had packed in her job and was leaving Solihull, as she had believed then, forever. On Falco's desk she had left a plain buff envelope that contained her diamond and sapphire engagement ring and a cryptic note, dictated by his father, telling him that she no longer loved him.

He would never believe it, she'd told herself firmly, over and over again through the sobs that shook her on that endless, nightmare journey down to London. He'll know it's a lie, that his father has made me do this. He'll come looking for me, and, because he's Falco, he'll find me.

And so, down in London in her St John's Wood retreat, she had waited, each day a living torment, praying with all her strength that today would be the day. And though at times she had almost been driven mad by anguish, she had never stopped believing that he would find her.

And six agonisingly long weeks later he had.

One day she had stepped out of the St John's Wood apartment block to see Falco striding across the street towards her.

But what had happened next had almost destroyed her.

Accusations. Foul and bitter accusations.

'Bitch!' he had called her. 'You disgust me!' he had yelled at her. 'I've always known there were people who'd do anything for money, but I didn't know until now that you were one of them!'

She'd been speechless at first. Uncomprehending. 'What are you talking about?' she'd demanded, close to weeping.

'The money you took!' He'd waved at the luxury flat block. 'The money you took from my father to pay for all of this!'

She'd been about to deny it. The very thought was too horrible. But then he had been shouting at her again, his face contorted with terrible anger.

'You're nothing but a tramp! I saw you with your new boyfriend. I saw you this morning climbing into his Jaguar. You didn't wait long to replace me, did you? Straight out of one bed and into another!'

In that instant it had been as though she was looking at a stranger. He *was* a stranger, if he could believe such vile things of her. She knew who the man was that Falco was referring to, and he could in no way whatsoever be described as a boyfriend.

As she hesitated, Falco had blazed at her, 'Go on, try to tell me it isn't true!'

But Laura had shaken her head, her heart frozen within her, and stared with icy eyes at the stranger before her. She would not stoop to denying what should need no denial. If that was what he thought of her, let him think it.

In a state of shock she had heard herself telling him, 'I'm glad I took the money and got shot of you! And my new boyfriend's bed is much more exciting than yours.' Then she'd stood and watched, her body turned to stone, as with an angry oath he had turned and walked away.

That was the last time she had set eyes on him until she had walked into the sun-filled sitting-room, just a few hours ago, and seen him standing by the window. But they had been in touch, once, since then. There had been the letters.

Laura sighed and rose slowly from the dressing-table chair. That letter she had sent him, a year and a half ago, might have caused him to believe that she was still in love with him. It could explain that taunt about the supposed 'problem' she was suffering from.

A small laugh escaped her lips. He must be crazy! She had stopped loving him that day outside the St John's Wood flat! She'd sent the letter in a fit of madness, with the intention of sharing her secret with him. In her madness she'd felt he had a right to know.

'There are certain things I'd like to discuss with you,' she'd written. 'Perhaps we could arrange a meeting some time?'

His reply had come back to her a couple of weeks later. Brief. Discourteous. 'We have nothing to discuss.'

She had known then that she'd been wrong. He had no right to share her secret. She'd been a sentimental fool ever to have believed he had.

A sentimental fool and a foolhardy one, too, she thought to herself now as a shiver went through her. If she had revealed her secret she might have ended up losing what was most precious to her in all the world.

Her daughter. Their daughter. Hers and Falco's. Her beautiful Belle who lit up her life.

She shivered again. Knowing Falco, if he ever found out about his daughter, he might come and try to take her away. Just out of spite. For no other reason. That was her nightmare. For she knew that would destroy her.

And that was why she could not ignore his threat to go to London and start discussing her with her colleagues. All of them knew about her daughter. One or two even knew that Belle's father was someone Laura had known, a long time ago, back in Solihull. It would take just one careless word and her secret would be out.

She could not risk that. And so she had agreed to stay. In order to keep her secret safe.

On a surge of determination, pushing her fear from her, she crossed to the wardrobe and, with a defiant flourish, pulled out the most colourful dress she had brought with her.

She must be strong. For he knew nothing. She was certain. The only real danger was that her own anxiety would trick her into betraying herself.

Taking a deep breath, she slipped the dress from its hanger. She *would* be strong. She would hold on tight to her secret. Falco, until the day he died, would never know he had a daughter.

CHAPTER THREE

'AN APERITIF? Gin and tonic—your usual?'

'Did that used to be my usual? I couldn't have told you. But, if you don't mind, I'd prefer a Campari and soda.'

Did that sound churlish? Too self-consciously distancing? Laura suspected it probably did, for he was absolutely right, gin and tonic in the old days had been her 'usual'. And it was a drink she still enjoyed and might even have opted for had Falco not made the fatal mistake of assuming he was still in tune with her preferences.

He was in tune with nothing about her. They were as good as total strangers. The Laura who stood before him now was not the Laura he had accused and lied to three years ago.

But he seemed not to have noticed the rebuke in her response. 'Good idea,' he observed, deepening her irritation. 'I think I'll have a Campari and soda, too.'

Laura turned away from him to face the french windows, which stood open, allowing the thin thread of a breeze that drifted up from the seafront to gently ruffle the pale curtains.

They were in the main sitting-room, which overlooked the gardens that stretched down through the scented air to the palm-fringed beach. Falco had been waiting for her here, dressed in a dark suit and silk tie, when she had come down for dinner just a few minutes ago, looking bright and confident in her poppy-coloured dress. There were just the two of them. There was no sign of Janine.

Laura glanced up at the moon and hoped the girl would show up soon. Being alone with Falco was not something she relished.

'Shall we step outside? Take a breath of fresh air? It's very pleasant at this time of the evening.'

All at once, surprising her, he was standing at her elbow, holding out to her the tall glass of bright red Campari.

'If you like.' Laura almost snatched the glass from his hand and stepped quickly out on to the patio that bordered the garden. His nearness unsettled her. She found it unpleasant.

There were white-painted wrought-iron tables and chairs arranged on the patio beneath a spreading fig tree. 'Shall we sit?' Falco suggested, waving towards them.

Laura nodded. 'Yes, why don't we?'

Falco pulled out a chair for her.

Laura seated herself stiffly. They were behaving like strangers. And she found that precisely to her satisfaction. That was exactly the way things ought to be!

'So, what's the final verdict?' Taking a sip of his drink, Falco had seated himself in one of the chairs opposite her. Laura found it oddly comforting that the iron table stood between them.

She regarded him across the top of it. 'The final verdict about what?'

'About whether or not you plan to honour your commitment to decorate my villa for me.'

'I've already told you I've decided to do it.'

'Ah, yes. But that was a couple of hours ago.' He regarded her across the table with mocking amusement. 'When dealing with someone who is as prone as you are to sudden, inexplicable changes of mind, it is advisable to take absolutely nothing for granted.'

'I am prone to no such thing.'

'That has not been my experience.'

The mocking amusement in his eyes had vanished. He sliced the accusation across at her like a whiplash.

Laura held her breath a moment. Suddenly they were no longer strangers. Suddenly, like barbed wire, their angry past ensnared them. But she answered in a cool tone,

'The experience you're referring to has no bearing on the current situation. As I've told you before, in matters of business you can rely on me absolutely.'

'That is indeed reassuring.' He regarded her scathingly. 'But then I have long been aware of that side of your character—that you do the work you're paid for, however dishonourable it may be.'

Laura winced, but managed to hide it. He must never have truly loved her, must never have understood her to have accepted that lie so totally.

She looked back at him, her gaze steady as he continued, 'But what I happen to be wondering at this moment is, can one count on this somewhat selective reliability of yours before money has changed hands ... or only after?'

Again she winced, but hid it. 'You needn't concern yourself. In matters of business, as I've already told you, my word is absolutely iron-clad.'

'Because I can give you a cheque up-front, if you want.'

'I can assure you that won't be necessary.' Hadn't he heard her? 'I shall present you with my bill when the work has been completed.'

'You're absolutely sure?'

'Absolutely. Thank you.'

She looked into his face with its dark steel-hook eyes. He was determined to torment her. Was that why he had brought her here? To take vengeance for all the wrongs he liked to pretend she had done him?

Perhaps, she decided. It was a more convincing explanation than his claim that it was pure chance that had landed her on his island.

'What about your expenses during the initial two weeks? It would be no problem for me to give you some cash in advance.'

'My expenses, I imagine, will not be very great. After all, I shall be eating and sleeping here.' She paused and glanced across at him. 'While we're on the subject . . . I know the agreement I made with Janine was that I should spend a couple of weeks here, getting to know the house, then go back to London to complete a small job I have there before returning here to get down to work . . .' She looked him in the eye. 'I think two weeks is too long. One week would be quite sufficient.'

'I disagree.'

She had anticipated that. Still she pressed her case. 'I wish you'd accept my judgement. One week really would be quite sufficient.'

'As I said, I disagree.' He took a mouthful of Campari and subjected her to a long black glittering look. 'I have specifically taken two weeks off in order that I can spend it with my decorator, making sure she gets to know the house in all its different moods, and discussing with her the different ideas she may have.'

Ice touched Laura's heart. She felt herself shiver.

'You mean you intend to be actively involved in this project?'

'Of course.'

'I didn't know that. I thought Janine was in charge.'

'The house is mine.'

'It was she who hired me.'

'But it is I who will be paying you.'

'I realise that, but——'

Falco cut her short. 'And I'm the one you'll be dealing with.' The dark eyes bored through her, seeming to see what she was feeling. 'What's the matter? Is this iron-clad reliability of yours suddenly wavering at the prospect? Do you feel unable to cope with two weeks of my company?'

He really did think she had a problem with that. And she did. But not for the reason he believed. Not because he still had an emotional hold on her. She simply found the prospect of two weeks with him repellent.

She said, 'Why on earth should I find that a problem? Do you plan on being difficult to cope with?'

'Am I ever?' He smiled with irony.

'I have no idea.' She looked back at him steadily. 'I have no experience of you in professional matters.'

'Then you're about to get some now.' His eyes drove through her. He smiled an irritating smile. 'A whole two weeks of it.'

'I see. You're not prepared to accept my professional judgement that two weeks is unnecessarily long?'

'I am not. Two weeks is what you agreed to in London.'

In all innocence, she had, though her tender mother's heart had wept at the thought of two weeks' separation from her daughter. But, alas, she'd been in no position to refuse. A lucrative commission had just recently fallen through and she had bills to pay. She needed the money.

And, besides, she'd known that Belle would be well looked after while she was gone. Her adoring grandparents had literally jumped at the chance of a visit to London to help her nanny look after her. And two-year-old Belle had been delighted with the arrangement. As much as they adored her, their secret grandchild, Belle adored her grandparents every bit in return.

So now, though she honestly believed it was too long, it looked as though Laura would have to stick with her original agreement. In a wry tone she told Falco, 'Very well, then. If you can stand it, I guess I can, too.' She raised her glass ironically and took a mouthful of her Campari. 'It looks as if you win. Two weeks it is.'

It was at that moment that Janine appeared in the patio doorway, wearing a puckered little frown and very little else. The négligé that was wrapped around her slender suntanned body was so fine you could have rolled it up and stowed it in your

pocket—and still have had room for your wallet
and keys.

In a small, plaintive voice, she was demanding,
'Falco, darling. Can I have a word?'

Falco darling did not need to be asked twice.
With an alacrity that Laura found oddly jarring,
he was jumping to his feet and hurrying towards
her.

'What is it, Janine?' There was real concern in
his voice. He caught Janine by the elbow and steered
her back into the drawing-room. Laura caught the
murmur of half-whispering voices as the two of
them disappeared from sight.

And quite suddenly she was aware of a violent
pounding inside her. An eruption of emotion so
unexpected and so fierce that just for a moment
she could scarcely breathe.

It was the way he had spoken, the gentleness in
his face, the warmth he had exuded as he had
hurried to Janine. She had forgotten that side of
him—the compassion, the caring, the kindness with
which he could be so unstinting. To see it manifest
now, in so spontaneous a fashion, had filled her
with an overwhelming sense of grief for what was
lost and so momentous.

Laura took a sharp breath and strove to compose
herself. Was she out of her mind? What was there
to grieve for? And besides, she'd done grieving a
long time ago.

By the time Falco reappeared in the doorway,
Laura's poise had returned. She felt calm and in
control again. She felt not a flicker of any emotion
whatsoever as he paused for a moment, his dark
eyes seeming to scrutinise her, before informing with

an almost provocative smile, 'Janine is feeling poorly. She's gone to her room. So it looks as though it'll just be the two of us for dinner.'

'How delightful.' Laura looked back at him and parodied a smile. Then with rather more sincerity she added, 'I hope it's nothing serious. Janine, I mean.'

'No, nothing serious. Just a migraine.' As he spoke, he remained standing in the doorway. 'No doubt she'll have recovered fully by tomorrow.' Then he straightened slightly. 'Dinner's ready, by the way. Shall we go through to the dining-room?'

Laura drained her Campari and rose to her feet, quelling the spurt of annoyance she felt at the prospect of dining alone with Falco. She must not allow the situation to annoy her. Indifference, not annoyance, that was what she must strive for.

Falco led her through the huge high-ceilinged drawing-room to a panelled oak door that led to the dining-room, where, beneath a shimmering crystal chandelier, stood a table set with gleaming glass and silver.

Laura paused and looked around her, mentally taking notes. Already she could feel the stirrings within her of ideas for the villa's eventual transformation.

It was as though he'd read her mind. 'I'd like to keep the chandelier. But most of the other contents of the room can go.'

'I'll bear that in mind.' Laura did not glance at him. His suggestion was precisely what she herself had been thinking and she found it irksome in the extreme that they could be in agreement about anything.

The third place at the white-clothed rectangular table had with remarkable efficiency already been cleared away. There were just two places now, one at the head of the table, the other on its immediate left.

'Take a seat.'

Falco waved her towards the second place, as he pulled out his own chair at the head of the table. And Laura could not resist it. As she seated herself, she glanced across at him. 'No doubt, when it comes to replacing the table, your preference will remain with the rectangular variety. A round table poses such problems for the head of the household.'

'I couldn't agree more. Far too democratic.'

'Quite unsuited to the male Roth temperament.'

There was a momentary pause. He had not expected that barb. 'Is that how you see me? As a typical male Roth?' He sounded amused. There was not a flicker of shame.

'Why, isn't that what you are?'

Isn't that what you have become?

She very nearly asked that second question. But she was glad she hadn't. It would have been misleading. After all, she knew that it was not that he had changed, but rather that, in the beginning, she had been fooled by the gentle mask.

In the beginning she had believed he was not a typical male Roth. Quite unlike his ruthless father and his legendary equally ruthless grandfather. But the men in the Roth family were all the same. How grateful she had always been that her child had been born a girl.

Falco allowed her question to remain unanswered as Anna appeared in the doorway, carrying a steaming tureen. But his eyes were on Laura as the dark-haired woman proceeded to ladle the soup into their plates. As Anna set down the tureen and retreated discreetly, he observed calmly, as though there had been no interruption, 'If you mean am I hard-working, dedicated, ambitious and highly successful at what I do, I suppose the answer to your question is yes. I am indeed a typical male Roth.'

Laura allowed herself a smile as she laid her napkin on her lap. How clever he was. How manipulative. How evasive. These attributes he had mentioned, as he knew perfectly well, were not the attributes to which she'd been referring.

She took a spoonful of her soup. 'I'm sure you're all of these things.' Then she raised her eyes to his and added in a tone whose calm indifference greatly pleased her, 'The Roth males, however, do have certain other attributes. Attributes which could be described as rather less endearing.'

'For example?'

She shook her head. 'I think you know what I'm talking about.' The prospect of a slanging match did not appeal to her.

Falco, however, had no such sensitivities. He insisted, 'Tell me. Tell me what you mean.'

Laura took a deep breath. 'Since you really want to know, I would say the Roth males on the whole are better known for their hardness than for the attributes you describe. Their hardness, their ruthlessness, their lack of humanity. I'm sorry,' she added insincerely, 'if that offends you.'

'Why should it offend me? You're entitled to your opinion.' Falco bestowed on her a look of total condescension. Then he smiled a hard smile. 'But they can also be generous. That, surely, is a point to which you would be willing to testify?'

A coldness touched her. 'When it suits them,' she answered quietly.

Falco raised one dark eyebrow. 'When it suits *them*?' he repeated. 'That strikes me as a novel interpretation. Generosity, I would say, as a rule suits both parties. Both the party who extends it and the party who receives it.' He finished his soup and laid down his spoon. 'It certainly seemed to suit you pretty well. It allowed you to embark on a whole new life.'

Laura flashed him a look, as hard as she could muster. It still crushed her that he could believe she had taken that money. Defiantly, she responded, 'The changes in my life initiated by your father were the making of me. I wouldn't deny it.'

And that much was true. If Oscar Roth hadn't forced her to leave Solihull for London three years ago, professionally, she might never have become the success she was today.

The door opened again and Anna appeared, pushing a trolley laden with steaming platters. She laid the dishes before them—veal with mushrooms, buttered courgettes and baby potatoes—and filled their glasses from a bottle of ice-cold Verdicchio.

As they were left alone again, they ate in silence for a moment. Then Falco said, mock conversationally—for Laura caught the lacerating bite in his tone, 'Talking of generosity and those whom it suits to receive it... Do you still have that flat in St John's Wood?'

Laura looked back at him. 'No, I moved from there some time ago. I bought a place of my own in Primrose Hill.'

'A very nice area.'

'Yes, I like it.'

'Not quite as exclusive as your previous address, of course.'

'No, not quite,' she agreed. Inwardly, she was seething. What was going on inside that twisted black mind of his? 'You realise, of course, that the St John's Wood flat never actually belonged to me?'

Falco laughed. 'Oh, yes, I've always known that. There are definite limits to my father's generosity, even when faced with a hard bargainer like you.' He took a mouthful of his wine, laid down his glass and looked at her. 'To be honest, I've always thought it was quite extraordinarily extravagant of you to have rented a place like that in the first place. The rent must have eaten up a fair chunk of your capital.'

He had it all figured out! He'd probably even gone to the trouble of finding out what the rental of such an apartment would be. And it was despicable the way he'd spied and pried into her affairs and single-mindedly come up with all the wrong conclusions. He really was just an evil replica of his father!

But there was a perverse pleasure to be had in misleading him further. Laura chewed on a slice of courgette before putting to him, 'What appears to an outsider to be an extravagance can sometimes, in fact, prove to be a pretty shrewd investment.' She paused, feeling pleased with her choice of the word 'outsider', and then added, 'And my case, one might say, illustrates that perfectly.'

'Is that so?' He cut a slice of veal. It was clear he had no intention of pressing her to elaborate.

But Laura intended to tell him anyway. She wanted it on the record that she had carved out her career through hard work and talent, and not because Falco's father had financed her.

'There were a lot of very wealthy people living in that block of flats. The sort of people who hire professional decorators and give them their head. I passed the word round that I was a decorator and one of the other residents hired me to do up her flat. I made such a good job of it that as soon as her friends saw it commissions started pouring in from all over the place.'

'Good for you.'

'Yes, that's what I thought.' And that, in fact, was more or less what had happened.

More or less. She had excluded certain vital details. But to include them would only send her sliding down the long slippery slope of explanations and revelations of things he didn't want to know. And which she had not the slightest wish to tell him.

There was a small silence while they both ate, then Falco said, raising his eyes to hers, 'I always knew, of course. I always said you'd do it.'

'Do what?' Laura blinked at him. Surely she had misunderstood? That had sounded suspiciously like a compliment!

But it appeared she had not been mistaken, after all. Falco looked back at her unblinkingly. 'I always said you'd make it big. At least you can't deny that. I always had faith in your abilities.'

Laura was almost struck dumb. She looked into his face and seemed to see again, shining from his eyes, that look of total faith and unstinting encouragement that in the beginning had contributed so much to her own belief in herself.

She said quietly, 'No, I would never deny that.' She could hear her heart beating. The room all around her seemed suddenly to be filled by an eerie, echoing silence.

A long moment ticked by. Laura could feel his eyes on her. Then he said, and his tone had barely altered, 'Are you still seeing that young man?'

Laura frowned and shook her head. 'What young man are you talking about?'

Another long pause, then Falco answered. And this time there was an unmistakable edge to his voice. 'The one with the gaudy tie and the Hitler moustache.'

'No.' In an instant the spell was broken. Laura all at once could feel her stomach churning inside her. All at once she was standing outside the St John's Wood flat and he was hurling at her those crude accusations of infidelity.

She felt again the helplessness and the betrayal she had felt then, for of course there had been no new lover in her life, and certainly not that sleazy antiques dealer, with whom she'd had nothing more than reluctant business dealings.

And again she wondered, as she had wondered then, how Falco could jump to such a damning conclusion on what, after all, was no evidence at all.

But with an effort she managed to control these feelings. She went on to elaborate, her tone meticulously casual, 'I haven't seen him for a long time, as it happens. You know how it is? Things end. People drift apart.'

'In your world, yes, I believe that's how it is.' His tone was like a knife cutting into her. 'No doubt you found him useful for a while, then, when you got a better offer, you simply discarded him?' Before she could answer, he added callously, 'Did you manage to wangle a pay-off with that one as well?'

That was too much. Something snapped inside her. Laura laid down her cutlery. She could feel her heard pounding, as though it might suddenly burst out of her chest.

She said, 'And what if I did? What damned business is it of yours?' Her tone was suddenly as taut as piano wire, her careful indifference all blown away. 'My life, past and present, has nothing to do with you! Any stake you ever had in it ended three years ago! So kindly get that into your head once and for all!'

She had half risen in her seat, propelled by her anger. She remained poised there now, fury blazing from her, as Falco looked back at her, his features still, his dark eyes shuttered.

Then he stunned her totally.

'In that case,' he put to her, 'if, as you say, it all ended three years ago, how come you took the trouble to write to me eighteen months ago?' His tone was as cold and impersonal as an executioner's. 'How come you were so keen to set up a meeting?'

Laura felt her heart stop. That foolish letter. She swallowed, for a moment unable to speak.

'You said there were things you wanted to discuss. That doesn't sound to me like the sort of thing one writes to someone who no longer has a place in one's life . . .' He paused. 'What was it you wanted to tell me?'

Laura's vision had grown blurred. A sense of nausea swept through her. Did he know, after all? Did he even suspect? She could scarcely think straight for the panic that tore through her.

Her lips moved mechanically. 'Nothing,' she told him. 'There was nothing, really. Nothing important.'

'Then why bother to write? Why suggest a meeting?' His tone was quietly, mercilessly insistent.

Laura scrabbled in her brain for some kind of answer. She licked her dry lips. 'It was nothing important. I just wanted to set the record straight on certain matters.'

'But the record was already perfectly straight. As far as I can see, it couldn't have been straighter.'

'Yes, you made that clear in your reply.'

'And you were wasting your time if you'd been entertaining the thought that there was any possibility of me taking you back again.'

So, that was what he'd been thinking! That she'd been seeking his forgiveness! Relief tore through her. She managed a croaky laugh. 'Believe me, that was the last thing I was hoping for! Nothing could have been further from my mind!'

'So, what, if not to seek my forgiveness, was to be the purpose of our meeting?'

'I've already told you. Nothing at all.' Suddenly, Laura could not bear to pursue this conversation. She swung away awkwardly, almost toppling her chair. 'I'm going to bed. Janine had the right idea. You're enough to give anybody a migraine!'

But before she could step away, with the speed of a whiplash he had reached out one hand and caught her easily, his fingers closing around her wrist like a handcuff.

As she looked down at him, helplessly, he was smiling. 'I have a feeling I'm going to enjoy your little sojourn. It would appear, despite your protests, that we have unfinished business.'

Then he released her, and Laura could hear his mocking laughter follow her as she strode on paper legs from the room.

CHAPTER FOUR

THE water felt like cool slippery silk against her skin. Caressing, sensuous, sharpening her senses. With smooth strokes Laura cut her way through its glittering sapphire blueness, the still-gentle early-morning sun on her back, her head suddenly clearer than it had felt since her arrival on Alba.

She had slept badly last night, her brain full of ogres, ogres that pounded with bare-knuckled fists at the doors of memories long locked away. It had been a relief to get up just before seven, pull on her swimsuit, grab a towel from the bathroom and slip away from the still silently sleeping villa to indulge in an early-morning swim.

Now she could feel her tension springing away from her, like the tension in a guy rope suddenly released. With the grace of a seal, she rose up from the waves, head and shoulders exposed, shaking her water-bright hair, and raised her face to the warm slanting sun.

Damn Falco Roth! she thought with healthy vehemence. Damn him for ever having come back into my life! And damn him twice more for deliberately upsetting me!

She rolled over on to her back, her muscles relaxed, and allowed herself to float and bob like a cork. She had gone through enough agony for Falco Roth three years ago to last her a dozen miserable lifetimes. If she let him get to her again, and undermine her, she must be seriously crazy—which was one thing she was not!

Turning on to her front again, she swam a few more strokes, her slender body taut as it scythed through the clear blue water. What she was was a dedicated mother and career-woman, who had taken hold of her life over the past three years and achieved what was no less than a kind of miracle.

She had a wonderful little daughter, the apple of her eye, and a satisfying career that simply went from strength to strength. She had money in her pocket. A home of her own. And a social life that was full and satisfying.

No, she wasn't crazy. And she had every reason to believe in the strength of her own will and sense of purpose.

There was no man in Laura's life. There hadn't been since Falco. But that was a lack she was quite happy to live with. She had no desire for rash romantic involvements that in the end, inevitably, would come to nothing. She and Belle were far better off on their own.

Laura rolled over on to her back again and drank in the cool sea air. She had learned from the past. She had become her own person. And in a way, ironically, it was Falco she had to thank.

The bitter lesson he had taught her was that deep within her she possessed reserves of strength she had never before guessed at. She had discovered she could survive, even thrive, without him. She had learned she did not need him—or any other man.

Just for an instant she remembered again that terrifying moment, two weeks after their last meeting, when she had finally discovered that she was pregnant. She had feared then she would never find within herself the courage to cope with having a baby on her own. But she had. And what she had regarded initially with such terror had turned out to be the most joyful event of her life.

She laughed to herself now as with a quick flick of a somersault she turned herself over and headed back towards the shore. Falco was deeply misguided if he believed for one moment that she was still that fragile, gullible soul of before who had once gazed into his eyes, dreaming she saw her future there, too blind to realise that all she was seeing was lies.

Her arms sliced the water, powering her forward. He had said last night in that superior, arrogant way he had that he was looking forward to her sojourn, that they had unfinished business. His eyes had told her he planned to enjoy himself at her expense.

That was OK. Laura knifed through the sapphire water. Two could play at that little game. They had no unfinished business—he was mistaken about that—and she would take great pleasure in putting a damper on his fun!

Quite unintentionally, as it turned out, that was more or less the first thing she proceeded to do!

As she stepped from the water, Laura was suddenly aware of hunger pangs awakening inside her. She grabbed her towel from the sand where she had left it and rubbed her hair vigorously as she headed back to the villa—between the palm trees that fringed the beach edge and along the path that led through the garden. And she was virtually upon them before she was aware that she was intruding.

It was some sixth sense that caused her to glance up from her hair rubbing, as she stepped from the garden on to the edge of the patio. And there before her stood Falco and Janine, locked in a blissfully distracted embrace.

Janine's arms were round his neck, her brow bent against his chest, and she was smiling, laughing softly, as, arms circling her waist, Falco rested his chin against the top of her head, murmuring what were evidently welcome words of affection.

Welcome, but more than likely insincere, Laura found herself thinking with a curious tug at her heart.

She coughed discreetly to catch their attention. 'I beg your pardon. I didn't mean to disturb you.'

For some reason she had expected them to leap defensively apart. She had been anticipating, mischievously looking forward to, a display of shuffling embarrassment.

That did not happen. Two faces turned to look at her. Two faces that were composed and not the least bit embarrassed. No other part of the anatomy of either of them had moved.

Falco smiled. 'I hope you had an enjoyable swim?'

'Most enjoyable, thank you.' Laura felt faintly niggled—though she ought to have known, she reminded herself tartly, that Falco was not the type to be so easily wrong-footed. He had the gall of fifty men and the brass neck of a monkey.

She let her eyes swivel past him and glanced politely at Janine. 'I hope you've recovered from your migraine?'

It had been on the tip of her tongue to say, I *see* you've recovered . . . But that would have sounded bitchy, she realised, surprised at herself. She had no reason in the world to be bitchy to Janine.

Janine uncurled her slim brown arms from Falco's neck and let her hands slide down to rest lightly on his shoulders, pausing on their way to make a totally unnecessary adjustment to the collar of the blue denim shirt he was wearing. Laura felt curiously irritated by this proprietorial fussing.

'Yes, thanks, the migraine's gone.' Janine made a small face. 'I'm sorry I wasn't able to have dinner with you last night.'

'That's all right. I quite understand. With a migraine the last thing one feels like being is sociable.'

Janine nodded. 'Too right. They're nasty, awful things. And, unfortunately, I seem to be rather prone to them.'

You should change the company you keep, Laura thought to herself privately. Falco Roth is enough to give anyone a migraine—which was more or less precisely what she had told him last night, she recalled, slipping him a look of furtive condemnation.

The look failed to connect. His gaze was focused on Janine. 'You *used* to be prone to them,' he was saying, his tone soft, one hand gently caressing her hair. 'That's a habit we're going to get you out of.'

'You're so sweet.' Wrinkling her nose, Janine kissed him on the chin. 'No one's ever been as sweet as you are to me before.'

Laura had watched the scene with oddly mixed feelings. Part of her wanted to laugh with derision. Once, she too had known this soft seductive side of him and had learned just how false it was. It was a cynical performance.

But how could she laugh when it was perfectly obvious that poor Janine was totally taken in—as she had been once—and was clearly deeply vulnerable? Through the angry contempt she felt for Falco her heart went out in sympathy to the girl.

She said, wishing to excuse herself, her stomach churning with emotion, 'I think I'll go and change now. Then I'll find myself some breakfast.'

'No need to change.' As she was about to hurry past them, Falco swiftly disengaged himself from Janine's embrace and stepped back, as though deliberately to block Laura's path.

'And you can have breakfast here. The table's all ready.' He gestured to one of the tables beneath the fig tree. 'Anna will be bringing us breakfast any minute.'

'I'll change first, if you don't mind.' Laura was annoyed. For Janine's sake, not her own. He was standing far too close to her, his eyes openly appraising her semi-naked body, lithe and curvaceously female in the clinging wet swimsuit.

She was about to flash him a hard, condemning look, but suddenly, as she looked at him, her attention was caught by the tiny dark mole, half hidden in his lashes, at the outer corner of his left eye.

Laura had forgotten about that mole. She felt her heart shift strangely. Once, foolishly, it had been one of the things that made him special. Once she would kiss it and watch him smile as she did so.

Momentarily, the memory filled her with distress. It seemed impossible and almost heartbreaking that things could once have been so different.

She tore her gaze away with a dart of impatience at herself and focused determinedly on her annoyance. 'Kindly excuse me,' she demanded.

He stepped back then, but still smiling, unrepentant. 'Consider yourself excused. We'll see you later.'

Insensitive swine! Laura stormed past him across the patio. No wonder poor Janine was prone to headaches. No woman—and certainly not one as insecure as Janine—enjoyed watching her man eyeing up another woman!

Up in her room Laura showered quickly. Then she combed back her hair—she would allow it to dry naturally—and slipped on a simple blue cotton shift dress and pushed her feet into matching strappy sandals. A couple of minutes later she was hurrying downstairs again, her stomach growling an urgent demand for breakfast!

And yet, as she stepped out on to the patio, she paused, her appetite momentarily fleeing. Falco sat alone at the table beneath the fig tree, a cup of coffee in his hand, a half-eaten croissant on his plate.

Laura squared her shoulders as she crossed the patio to join him. 'What's happened to Janine?' she enquired.

'She had things to do. And she said she wasn't hungry.'

As he glanced up at her and smiled, Laura suddenly had the feeling that he had contrived this cosy breakfast *à deux*. She sensed he had sent Janine away so he could have her to himself. What exactly was he playing at? she wondered.

She seated herself. No doubt she was about to find out.

'Did you sleep well?' He pushed the coffee-pot towards her and indicated that she should help herself to croissants and *brioches*, the sweet rolls that were such an essential part of any Italian breakfast.

Laura poured herself a big cup of *caffè latte*—strong espresso coffee with creamy hot milk—and lied without compunction. 'I slept like a log.'

'Me, too. But then, I always do. Especially when I'm here. It's the sea air that does it.'

Laura's interest in the quality of Falco Roth's sleep, on a scale of one to ten, rated about zero. Casually, she helped herself to a *brioche* and observed with what she hoped was not too apparent a sense of satisfaction, 'What a pity you can only enjoy such pleasures rarely. I expect you don't manage to spend as much time here as you'd like?'

'On the contrary, I manage to spend quite a lot of time here. Otherwise, I wouldn't have bought the villa.'

He sounded sickeningly self-satisfied. Laura picked up her knife and sliced open her *brioche* a little more violently than was necessary. But her tone was as sweet as barley sugar as she put to him, 'I hope that doesn't mean you're neglecting your duties at Roth Engineering? That would be most ungrateful of you, considering all it's done for you.'

By now, no doubt, he had risen up the hierarchy in the footsteps of his abominable father. At the very least, she felt certain, he would have a seat on the board.

Falco leaned back in his chair, brown arms folded across his chest. 'Was I ever,' he enquired lightly, 'one to neglect my duties?'

'Professionally speaking, I suppose the answer is no.' You always knew, she might have elaborated, on which side your bread was buttered. His attachment to the family firm had not been out of passion. He had once told her it was out of a sense of duty. But the real truth, she suspected, was that it was out of self-interest.

'Only professionally speaking?' He had picked up her reservation. 'Do you consider that my sense of duty extends no further than that?'

Laura shrugged and conceded, her tone censorious, 'I suppose you were always a most dutiful son.'

'Isn't that what sons are supposed to be—dutiful? Sons, and daughters, too, come to that.'

Laura had been spreading her *brioche* with a thin layer of butter. But suddenly her hand had frozen over the knife. She looked up into his face, feeling that familiar sense of fear in her.

'Daughters?' she repeated, feeling her heartbeat inside her, not daring to wonder what he had meant.

'Daughters, yes.' He held her eyes a moment. Then he added, 'After all, you yourself, as I remember, were always a most diligent and dutiful daughter.'

Again that rush of relief. Laura laid down her knife with fingers that were stiff from disguising their trembling. His reference to daughters had been a chance remark. Laura breathed in deeply and spoke to herself sternly. I must stop reacting this way to every little thing or I shall die of a heart attack before the fortnight's out!

'So, why,' he continued, unaware of her turmoil, 'do you sound so critical of me for being a dutiful son?'

'Some fathers...' She looked at him, then abruptly snatched her eyes away. Just for an instant she had felt a flash of something—something that had felt illogically like guilt—that he was ignorant, and would remain so, of his paternal state. 'Some fathers,' she continued, keeping her eyes on her *brioche*, 'don't deserve to have dutiful offspring.'

'I see.' He was looking back at her. Laura could feel his eyes on her. 'And my father, in your estimation, belongs in that category?'

Laura shrugged. 'Yes, frankly, that would be my opinion. But of course you know your father better than I do. You must have had good reason for always defending him as you did.'

'Did I?'

'Oh, yes. On many occasions. You used to refuse to listen to a bad word against him.'

She raised her eyes to his, then, and looked into his face. Surely he would not have the gall to deny her accusation? 'Whenever people criticised your father—friends, acquaintances, workmates, whatever—you used to get absolutely furious. I even remember you threatening to beat one guy up!'

'How very melodramatic of me. And did I do it?'

'Do what?'

'Keep my threat? Beat him up?'

'No, he backed down, just as they always did.'

In spite of herself, a complimentary smile touched Laura's lips. She felt a twist of remembered admiration, almost pride. Few people, even men who were twice his size, had ever had the nerve to stand up to Falco. And not simply because of his strong physique—for he had always been a super-fit and powerfully built man—but rather because of the mental steel one sensed in him. He had the power to dominate with a flash of those dark eyes.

She shook her head inwardly. In the old days she had believed that that core of steel in him was employed, on balance, more in the service of the angels than of the devil.

That had been before the scales had fallen from her eyes.

The devil's equerry was pouring himself a fresh cup of coffee. 'So,' he observed calmly, as though they were discussing the weather, 'we have established that I am not lacking in a sense of duty, either professionally or with regard to my father.' He fixed her with a look. 'Yet you seem to be hinting that in some unspecified department a sense of duty is definitely lacking.'

'Am I?'

'I have that feeling.'

Laura shrugged. 'Then you're mistaken.'

It would be wise, she was thinking, to cut this conversation short before she was drawn into saying things she might later regret. For what did it matter now the sense of betrayal she had felt at the unhesitating way in which he had condemned her three years ago? It had been his duty, if he had loved her, to seek out the truth.

Rage flickered inside her. But that was the point. He had never loved her. He had only pretended.

But as she bit into her *brioche*, he persisted, 'I sense there's something you're holding back.'

'Do you?' In a clipped tone.

'Yes. I sense it strongly.'

'Then all I can say is that your senses are not to be trusted. I would strongly advise you to pay them no heed.'

'They always used to be pretty reliable—particularly where you and I were concerned.'

Laura's breath caught. It was as though he had trodden on her heart. He had no right to refer to what had once been between them. He had forfeited that right the day he had turned against her.

She took a deep breath and turned stony eyes on him. 'Does Janine know about our former...?' She paused in mid-sentence, her mind scrabbling to find a palatable word. 'Acquaintanceship,' she finished. It was the blandest she could come up with.

Falco drank some of his coffee, eyeing her over the cup's rim. He seemed amused by her verbal dilemma.

'You mean,' he challenged her, laying down his cup again, 'does Janine know that you and I were once lovers?'

Again Laura's breath caught. Her lips thinned with annoyance. She narrowed her eyes at him. 'That's what I said.'

'Did you?' He smiled across at her, dark eyes mocking. 'I know you said my senses were not to be trusted, but I had no idea that included my sense of hearing. I distinctly thought I heard you use the word "acquaintanceship".

'Such an impersonal word.' He held her eyes across the table. 'I wondered if you might have conveniently forgotten that there was a great deal more to our relationship than was implied by your somewhat impersonal choice of word. I therefore took it upon myself to remind you.'

Laura clenched her jaw tight to stop herself from saying the words she felt rising spontaneously to her lips. I had not forgotten, she'd been on the point of answering. But suddenly, inexplicably, she'd been deeply afraid of what she might reveal through these four innocuous words.

Her eyes, her tone of voice, she sensed, would betray her. How could I forget, they might have told him, the one and only love I have ever had?

She let a moment pass to calm her beating heart. 'You haven't answered my question,' she reminded him tightly. 'Have you told Janine about us?'

'What's to tell? What's past is past. It has no bearing on the present.'

'I disagree.'

'Funny, I thought you might.' He leaned towards her, elbows on the table, a speculative lift to his straight black eyebrows. 'I keep getting the impression that for you the past isn't past.'

Laura looked into his eyes. He really did believe that he still had some kind of emotional hold on her.

She told him brusquely, 'Don't be ridiculous. I'm simply suggesting that there's something rather odd about the fact that you apparently haven't told your girlfriend about our former relationship. I would say that's the sort of thing she has a right to know. Especially since I'm a guest in your house!'

'Now it's my turn to disagree. My relationship with you, past or present, I consider to be, quite categorically, none of Janine's business.'

That was faintly shocking. 'You really mean that?' Laura had the renewed sense, intensified, that he was a total stranger.

'Absolutely. I really mean it.'

As she continued to stare at him with hostile, narrowed eyes, he continued, 'Now that I've answered that question for you, let's go back to the other subject we were discussing... Your attitude to the past... and whether or not for you it's past.'

'Of course it's past. Dead and buried.'

'Are you sure?'

'Quite sure. I couldn't be surer.'

His eyes roamed her face. 'Perhaps that's a pity.' Then his gaze drifted down to the thrust of her breasts beneath the thin cotton shift she was wearing. 'There were aspects of our past relationship that would bear renewing.'

Laura felt herself flush and then suddenly grow pale beneath the frankly sexual scrutiny. Her stomach twisted strangely. Outrage, she told herself. Outrage and anger. She glared into his face. But there was another emotion that burned as hotly as her anger. A sense of something illogically akin to disappointment.

She brushed it away and focused on the anger. 'You really have become a replica of your father!'

'I am my father's son.'

'Oh, yes, I've always known that! I've always known—at least I've known for a very long time—

that you're as ruthless and cold-hearted and as in-human as he is.' She paused to snatch a breath. 'But until this very moment I hadn't realised that you're also a faithless, immoral philanderer!'

Her voice rose, a little too loud, even to her own ears. 'Have you no shame, to make passes at me like that, right here in this house where your girl-friend's staying?'

'Was that a pass?' He was unmoved by her attack. 'Was that really a pass worth getting quite so hysterical about?'

He was right. She had overreacted. What had got into her? Laura's gaze shifted uncomfortably. 'It was a pass,' she insisted. 'And any pass, in the circumstances, I would say, is out of place.'

'What a highly moral line.' His tone was sar-castic. 'You appear to have altered your stance on such matters, or perhaps you're simply suffering from a bad case of double standards.'

Laura knew instantly to what he was referring. And, as always, the accusation cut her like a knife.

She rushed to defend herself. 'That's not a fair accusation! You and I were already finished before I...before I...'

'Before you climbed into bed with someone else. Don't be so coy about putting it into words. You weren't so coy when it came to actually doing it!'

Laura felt a wave of nausea sweep over her. How could he believe that? She had asked herself a thousand times. And as she looked into his face, so dark and closed against her, she was suddenly overcome by a fierce and desperate longing to cast aside caution and blurt out the truth.

But she stopped herself in time, appalled at her own reaction. She must tell him nothing. Not one single thing. The more falsehoods that stood between them, the safer was her secret.

She took a deep breath, forcing her voice to remain steady. 'That wasn't infidelity. You and I were already finished.'

'Were we?' His eyes narrowed. 'Are you absolutely sure of that? Are you absolutely sure I'd read your note before you climbed into bed with your new boyfriend? Are you absolutely certain that you got the timing right?'

He sat back in his chair with a violence that almost toppled it. 'Not that such niceties matter a damn anyway.' He flung his napkin down on the table, scattering the contents of the sugar bowl. 'Such intricacies of timing don't change anything. You remain what you are—a hard-necked bitch!'

'And you remain what you are—a bastard and a philanderer!'

Their eyes met and locked across the table, the blue and the black, driving into one another. And there was so much anger and emotion at that moment, gathered as tight as a fist in the air around them, that the ground beneath their feet almost seemed to tremble.

Then, suddenly, through the thunder a small voice was speaking.

'Is there any coffee left? Is it all right if I join you?'

Simultaneously, they glanced round to find Janine standing in the doorway, apparently unaware of the storm she'd stepped into. For an endless moment no one moved a muscle.

Falco recovered first. He rose to his feet. 'Come,' he was telling Janine. 'Come and sit down. I'll fetch some fresh coffee from the kitchen.'

Then without a glance in Laura's direction, as though he could not bear to be with her a moment longer, he was crossing the patio on angry striding steps and disappearing through the french doors into the villa.

Laura watched him go, struggling to control her breathing. She felt as though her lungs were full of splinters. Every inch of her body was as though gripped in a vice.

But what continued to appal her was the longing that still possessed her, that fierce, desperate longing to put an end to these falsehoods and finally to set him straight about what had happened in the past. Such longings were in direct and dangerous conflict with the need to keep her secret safe.

Through the pain that seized her heart, she felt her blood turn to ice.

What was happening to her? Was she going crazy, after all?

CHAPTER FIVE

IT TOOK Laura some time to recover her equilibrium. It was at least an hour before her heart-rate returned to normal.

Wisely, she'd made a point of leaving the breakfast table before Falco had time to return with the coffee. Wisely, for she was still afraid she might do something foolish.

'I'm sorry, I have to make a phone call,' she'd murmured to Janine, feeling discourteous, but knowing she had to escape. Her rationality, for the moment, appeared inexplicably to have deserted her.

Besides, it was true, she had to make a phone call. She'd promised to phone her parents and Belle every day, just to check that everything was OK.

And the phone call, she thought now, as she sat on her bedroom balcony, gazing out over the sunlit aquamarine sea, had done a great deal towards restoring her sanity. Belle was fine, and she and her grandparents were having a great time.

She smiled wryly to herself. If only I could say the same. If only I could rid myself of this tumult in my heart. If only things could go back to being the way they were.

Dead and buried. That was what she had believed the past to be. Forgotten. Behind her. Over and done with.

And now, here it was, tripping her up at every corner, opening old wounds, breaking her heart. And turning her into some kind of crazy woman.

Though, now that she was calm, she understood those dangerous longings that had almost caused her to blurt out the truth to Falco. It was the hate she'd seen in his eyes as he'd accused her, the hate she knew she did not deserve. It had been her sense of justice, nothing else, that had possessed her. And in the end she had overcome it. She had told him nothing. Her secret was still safe, protected by the wall of lies and misunderstandings that stood between them.

Yet for how much longer would it continue to be safe, she found herself wondering with a shiver, if Falco continued to throw the past, like gunpowder, in her face?

She sighed and closed her eyes. If only she could leave. Little had she realised, when she'd decided to stay, just what she was walking into.

And again she wondered: Was this why Falco had brought her here? To settle old scores? To eat his revenge cold? To repay her, with interest, for hurting his pride?

It looked that way. She breathed deeply and slowly. Which simply meant that she must continue to be strong. She must learn to expect and shrug off those attacks of his. That was the only way to survive.

And she would survive. Hadn't she always? She had the strength within her. She had proved that to herself.

After that little talk with herself, Laura felt much better. Once more in control of the situation. She stood up, left the balcony and went calmly downstairs.

A surprise awaited her down in the drawing-room.

As Laura hurried across the hall, she was aware of the sound of voices. Laughing voices. Conversation in full flow. She paused in the drawing-room doorway, not wishing to intrude. It would appear that, while she'd been upstairs, guests had arrived.

'Ah, there you are, Laura. Come in and join us!'

As though he really meant it, as though he were delighted to see her, Falco was rising to his feet and beckoning her into the room. From the smile on his face one could never have guessed at the bitter words he'd spoken to her just over an hour ago.

It had been Laura's intention to beat a subtle retreat. She had no desire to spoil the party. Falco, she had suspected, wouldn't want her around and it would be quite nice to have him out of her hair for a while anyway.

But she found herself stepping into the room, her head held high, a bright smile on her lips, and heading towards the little group with the confidence of one who was sure of her welcome. If he can fake it, so can I, she was thinking!

'This is Laura, my designer, all the way from London.' Falco took her by the elbow and drew her into the little group, executing the small gesture with such easy panache that even to Laura, for a split second, it seemed warm and genuine. 'Laura is going to transform the villa for me.'

The visitors were two young American couples. Alec and Josey and Bob and Marie. As Laura seated herself in the armchair next to Falco—where he had indicated she should sit—Josey told her, 'You lucky girl. I'd love to be in your shoes. I'd have a field-day decorating a fabulous house like this!'

Laura smiled. 'You're right. It is a fabulous house. What you might call a decorator's dream.'

'I'll bet!'

'I'm sure Laura's going to do wonderful things to it.' Falco glanced round at his guests and told them, 'Laura's one of the top designers in London.'

'How exciting!' Marie bubbled. 'You must meet all sorts of interesting people. Have you done up any palaces for princes or earls?'

Laura laughed. 'Not yet. I haven't quite hit that bracket. But you're right, I do meet a lot of interesting people.'

For some reason, as she said that, she was aware of Falco looking at her. She wondered if he was thinking of that sleazy antiques dealer, the one with the gaudy tie and the Hitler moustache. Inwardly, she cringed, expecting some cutting remark.

But he was smiling benignly. 'Laura's a very talented girl. I'm sure it's only a matter of time before she's asked to do up Buckingham Palace.'

It was a joke, but a kind joke. He had said it with a smile, as though he actually believed such a thing might be possible. And just for a moment Laura was thrown back to the old days when she had first dared to share all her secret ambitions with him and he had responded with unflinching faith and encouragement, suddenly making even her wildest dreams seem possible.

Just for a moment he seemed to shine before her eyes again. Just for a moment something flared up with pleasure inside her.

The conversation moved on. They chatted about this and that, and Laura found herself feeling more and more relaxed. Falco's friends, she learned, were doing a tour of Italy and were based for a few days at Pozzuoli, near Naples. They'd come to Alba on the off-chance, hoping to see Falco.

And it was precisely because she was feeling so relaxed that Laura proceeded to walk straight into a perfectly innocent trap.

It happened when Josey suddenly said, 'The only thing I regret about this wonderful holiday is that our little boy, Eddie, couldn't come with us. He's gone off to summer camp and I'm sure he's having a great time, but I really miss him. It's hard being without your kid.'

'Oh, I know how you feel!' Laura had spoken without thinking. Her heart slammed inside her. She felt her cheeks grow pale. And instantly, aghast, she rushed to cover herself. 'I mean I can *imagine* how you feel. It must be really hard.'

She didn't dare look at Falco, but she could feel his eyes on her. Had he picked up her slip? Had he put two and two together? She felt an inner rush of panic and fury at herself. Had she, out of carelessness, betrayed her secret?

If she had, she was not about to find out just yet. Alec spoke. 'I reckon it's time for lunch. Let's go catch that ferry and get back to the mainland. There's a great little *trattoria* near our hotel.'

'Will you be joining us, Laura?' It was Marie who was speaking to her. 'Come on. Be our guest. The more the merrier.'

Laura shook her head, keeping her eyes away from Falco. 'I have work to do here,' she said. 'I've hardly looked at the villa yet. But thanks all the same for the invitation.'

'You see what a dedicated decorator I have!' Falco made the remark lightly as they all rose to their feet, but Laura thought she detected a subtle edge to his tone, an edge that had not been there before.

She looked into his face, forcing a smile, searching his eyes for some hostile revealing glint. But she saw nothing to confirm her sudden clawing fear. The expression in the bright black eyes was inscrutable.

Perhaps I imagined it, she told herself, clutching at hope. Perhaps he didn't even notice.

Soon after that the others all left—the six of them, including Janine—and Laura prepared to spend a day exploring the villa. Exploring the villa and struggling not to dwell on the awful *faux pas* she had made.

But there was one thing she was sure of... Even if he confronted her, she would deny everything. He would never know the truth!

Laura had expected Falco and Janine to have returned by evening. But there was still no sign of them as she got ready to go to bed.

That's good, she decided. They're obviously having such a good time that they decided to stay overnight. In fact, they're obviously having such a good time that the last thing Falco's thinking of is my little slip.

She climbed between the sheets and lay back against the pillows, and suddenly, unsummoned, an image rose up in her mind. An image of Falco and Janine and the four Americans having a wonderful time together without her. For some crazy reason she found that image less than pleasing.

Fool, she chastised herself, rolling over and curling up. That's precisely what you want. That's precisely what can save you. What you want is that Falco has been so engrossed in his friends' company that he hasn't given you, or your little slip-up, another thought.

But that sense of displeasure, irritatingly, stayed with her. And, though it galled her, she sensed she knew the reason why. That brief time she had spent with him in the company of his friends, before they had all set off for the mainland without her, had reminded her of times spent together long ago, when she and Falco had meant so much to one another.

She crushed the thought impatiently. Who was she fooling? She had believed she meant a lot to him, but that had been a lie.

Anger stirred within her, making her feel better. She reached out quickly and switched off the light.

'I think it's time we did a tour of the villa together. Then we can have lunch and discuss your initial impressions.'

Laura swung round, startled at the sound of Falco's voice. She was in the library, where she'd been taking some measurements, and she hadn't heard him come into the room.

'Oh,' she said. 'You're back. I didn't know you were back yet.'

She felt curiously thrown as she looked up into his face. The oddest sensation had gone charging through her. A sensation that belonged to another time, another place.

'We got back just about an hour ago.' He was freshly shaved, freshly showered. His dark hair was wet. He bore the lingering scent of soap. 'Janine went straight to bed.' Falco smiled. 'She was exhausted.'

'So, a good time was had by all?'

It came out a trifle cuttingly. Which annoyed her intensely. What did she care if Janine was exhausted, or *why* she was exhausted, or where she was sleeping?

But that was precisely what she had wondered. In whose bed was Janine sleeping? In whose bed did she habitually sleep at the villa? It was the first time she had wondered it. She felt acutely ashamed of herself. She sleeps in Falco's bed, of course, she answered herself angrily.

'So, shall we begin our little tour?' Falco was leaning against the door-jamb, watching her, smiling, as though he could see inside her head. He was dressed in white trousers and an open-necked blue shirt. He looked as sharp as a needle and not tired in the slightest.

Laura focused on his face. At least she could be grateful for one thing. It was clearly not his intention to confront her about yesterday. Most probably she'd been right. He hadn't even noticed her slip.

She smiled a bright smile. 'Right. Where shall we start?'

'How about right here?' Falco glanced round the library with its bookcase-clad walls, dark-wood panelling and leather sofas. 'As it happens, this is one room I have very specific ideas about.'

Laura threw him a cautionary look. 'Not too specific, I hope? It's not going to work if you plan to tell me in minute detail precisely what I'm supposed to do.'

That was normally not something she would have said to a client—at least, not in such plain and graphic terms. Normally, she encouraged as much input as possible. After all, it was the client's house and he was going to have to live in it. It was essential that she did things to his taste.

Still, in this case, she was rather glad she'd said it, and in precisely such plain and graphic terms. Saying it had brought her hostility to him sharply back into focus. And that was good. It had been growing a little fuzzy round the edges.

Falco's hostility had never been in any such danger. He threw her a cool look. 'Don't worry,' he told her, 'I have no intention of doing your job for you. Considering how much I'm paying you, that would be a little foolish.' He smiled. 'Like buying a dog and then barking oneself.'

That was a neat way of putting it—and of putting her in her place. The remark, thanks to just the right derisory inflexion, had succeeded in reducing her to the status of a dog. And a dog, morever, that he had bought and paid for.

Laura met his eyes, her hostility now perfectly focused. 'Now that we've got that clear, perhaps you'd like to proceed?'

Falco's smile merely broadened. It amused him to taunt her. More and more she had the feeling that that was why he had brought her here.

He said, 'As I was saying, I have some ideas for this room. Let me show you what I mean.'

So saying, he dislodged his tall frame from the door-jamb and led her over into one corner of the room, where a packing case was standing, partially open. He pushed aside the lid and from among handfuls of polystyrene drew out a small gilt-framed picture.

He held it out to her. 'I'd like you to use this as your inspiration for the decoration of this room.'

Laura only just managed to hold back a gasp. Part delight, part surprise, part some deeper emotion. A recollection of the past. Sudden and powerful.

She took the picture from him, her hands a little unsteady. 'It's beautiful!' she breathed. 'Quite perfectly beautiful!' She gazed down at the Indian Moghul miniature, a mass of movement and bright subtle colour. She could feel the blood rushing and swarming inside her.

'I have a dozen or so.' Falco gestured at the packing case. 'I've spent the last few years scouring the auction rooms of Europe, painstakingly gathering them together.'

'I imagine you have. They're not so easy to come by—especially not examples of this high quality.' Laura's eyes were drinking in the exquisite beauty of the painting. It showed an Indian princeling and his retainers riding on elephants across a dazzling landscape. 'This must be one the most beautiful examples I've ever seen.'

'I've always had a passion for them. I love all the detail and the colour.' Falco smiled. 'This and the others are just the start of what I plan to be a sizeable collection.'

Laura almost said, I know. Had he forgotten? Three and a half years ago when he had taken her to her first auction in London the two of them had instantly fallen in love with a Moghul miniature not unlike this one. Falco had put in a bid, but the price had gone too high. In the end it had gone to an American buyer. But he had promised then that, one day, he would build himself a collection. And she had believed, just as she had believed every one of his promises.

She looked into his face now. Yes, he had forgotten. That happy day that had come flooding back to her so vividly at the sight of the picture she held in her hand was to him a meaningless long-forgotten thing. It had no more significance than a petal in the wind.

He was saying, 'How do you feel about designing the room around these pictures?'

'It'll be a pleasure.' Yet, though she smiled, her heart was aching. She was aware of a sense of near-total desolation. And that was utterly ridiculous, she reminded herself sharply. What didn't matter to him didn't matter to her either.

She handed the miniature back to him. 'I'll look at the others later.'

'Whenever you like. Feel free to examine them at your leisure.'

He hadn't moved, yet it seemed to Laura that he was closing in on her. His nearness was suffocating. And the way he was watching her. He seemed to be swallowing her up with his eyes.

She said, mock brightly, feeling suddenly stiff and awkward, 'Are there any other details you'd like me to keep in mind when I'm designing the décor for this room?'

'There's an Indian rug.' Still, he had not moved. 'Another of my auction-room finds. It's downstairs. I'll show it to you later.'

Laura nodded. 'Right.' She felt suddenly hot and cold. She wished he would move, but perhaps she was simply imagining that he was boxing her in against the packing case. Perhaps there was some other explanation for her sudden shortness of breath.

Still, the need to push him away was overpowering. So, afraid of being physical, she did it verbally.

'My, what a busy life you lead!' Her tone was edged with distancing harshness. 'I don't know how you manage to fit it all in. Dashing around to auctions all over Europe, holding down a senior position at Roth Engineering, and still with time left to spend on your Mediterranean island. I wouldn't have thought there were enough days in the week!'

She felt better instantly. That sense of closeness had receded. It had receded the instant she'd said the words 'Roth Engineering'.

Relieved, she proceeded to push him away further. 'Your father must have become more tolerant over the years. In the old days he used to be very demanding of your time.'

Falco's gaze had never flickered. His eyes were still on her. 'As you suggest,' he said quietly, 'things have indeed changed.'

'You've learned to get along? Oh, well, that's better for both of you.' That harsh edge to her voice had grown even harsher. Her whole body, from scalp to toe, felt stiff and hostile. 'And it's only to be expected. You're so like one another.'

'So you keep saying.' The dark eyes narrowed. In silence he scrutinised her face for a moment. Then he shifted slightly. 'I keep asking myself something... Perhaps you'd care to provide me with an answer. Why do you keep bringing up the subject of my father?'

'Do I?' Her heart fluttered.

'Surely you must be aware of it? At every opportunity you drag him into the conversation . . . as though you harboured some kind of grudge against him . . .'

'Do I?' She was being repetitious, but she could think of nothing else to say. Her mind had gone quite blank in the face of this unexpected inquisition.

Falco shook his head, frowning a little. 'It strikes me as odd . . . What kind of grudge could you be harbouring? After all, the only thing my father ever did to you was pay you a lot of money to walk out on me.'

Laura swallowed. 'Quite so.' She had shifted back away from him, so that the backs of her legs were now pressed against the packing case.

'So, what's the problem?'

'Nothing. I'm just being silly.'

'I would say you are. Unless there's something you're not telling me?'

'There's nothing I'm not telling you.' Her eyes, afraid to meet his, had fastened on the tiny mole in the corner of his left eye. She gazed at it fixedly, breathing slowly, struggling to control the rapid beating of her heart.

'You're quite sure about that?'

'Of course, I'm quite sure. I never liked him, that's all. You always knew that.'

Falco nodded. 'Yes, I did. But three years is a long time to go on hating someone who never did you any harm.'

'I suppose so. As I said, I'm just being silly...' She felt cornered against the packing case, the wood hard against her calves.

'Three years is a long time. I'm surprised you even remember him. In three years one can forget about almost anything.'

'Absolutely.' Her heart was thudding inside her. Her mouth felt dry. It was an effort to speak.

He was silent for a moment. A moment that stretched forever. Then he said, 'I, for example, had completely forgotten the way your cheeks go all pink when you're embarrassed.' He reached out with one hand and touched her pink cheeks. 'Like that time we bumped into each other in the corridor.'

Laura looked into his face then, her heart tight within her. She could neither speak nor move. She could scarcely even breathe.

'That's the way you look now.' Falco smiled as he said it, the fingers on her cheek curling round to cup her chin. 'You look as innocent and unworldly at this moment as you did that very first day we met.'

His eyes burned into her. 'Are you still that same girl? Beneath that poised, sophisticated exterior, are you still the same girl I remember?'

Laura wanted to push his hand away. She wanted to escape. She felt like his prisoner backed up against the packing case. But her limbs were frozen, her feet nailed to the floor.

Falco smiled. 'You intrigue me. Such beauty, such intelligence. Such an air of innocent sophistication...'

His thumb, as he spoke, brushed languorously against her lips, sending red-hot darts of sensation shooting through her.

She responded, a little croakily, 'What a ridiculous thing to say. I can assure you there's nothing the least bit intriguing about me.'

It might have been wiser to remain with her lips sealed. As she spoke, his thumb continued to stroke backwards and forwards, only now the sensations he was provoking were intensified as he took advantage of her unintentional collusion to gain access to the sensitive inner flesh of her lower lip.

Laura had forgotten the overpowering effect he could have on her. How the subtlest, most tentative physical contact between them could literally make her hair stand on end.

It was standing on end now. She could feel her scalp tingle. The power that flew from his fingers was electric.

With an effort of will she suppressed a shudder and spoke to herself sternly. What was she thinking of? This intimacy was outrageous. She must put an end to it at once.

Her muscles like lead, she raised one hand in protest and laid it on his wrist to push his hand away. 'Don't do that,' she told him. But even to her own ears the protest sounded unconvincing and puny.

'No? You don't like that?'

'I wish you'd stop it.' The hand she had raised to push away his hand remained, inexplicably, resting on his wrist.

'In that case I'll stop.' His hand slid away... to tangle instead with the the hair at the nape of her neck. He smiled down at her, a devil's smile. 'Do you like that better?'

'No, as a matter of fact, I don't.' Her whole body was on fire now. She made an ineffectual and what could only be described, she thought with shame, as a thoroughly half-hearted attempt to pull away. But his free hand had slipped round to encompass her waist.

'Falco, please!'

'Please what?'

'Please don't do that.'

'And what would you rather I did instead?'

His eyes drove into hers, as hot as burning coals. She felt excitement pour through her, disgraceful, forbidden. She tried to quench it, but it bubbled like a cauldron.

'Perhaps this is what you would really like me to do...?'

He was leaning closer. She could feel against her cheek his warm, sweet, tantalising breath. And she could sense, too, the power of the arms that embraced her and the muscular hard virility of the body that pressed against her.

And all at once Laura's heart was galloping uncontrollably. She knew he was going to kiss her and that she would do nothing to stop it. A welter of emotions were swarming through her. Horror, incredulity and a bitter-sweet yearning.

The world for one sharp moment seemed to tilt giddily on its axis. In her mind's eye Laura could see herself shoving him away, pulling herself free, putting an end to this madness. But the waters of temptation were already closing over her.

Involuntarily, her gaze shifted to that tiny dark mole, half hidden among his lashes in the corner of his left eye. And in that moment she knew the battle was lost. Her body sank against him, her hungry lips parting.

A moment later it was as though a typhoon had hit her. She seemed to be swept up from the ground where she had been standing, thrown like a rag doll into the air and simultaneously torn apart by a storm of sensuous feeling.

This was no simple kiss. Lips crushing against lips. This was no simple pleasure, like most kisses she had known. She felt the universe cry out. This was a collision of planets.

She had no choice but to cling to him or she might slip over the edge into a plummeting, dark oblivion. Her arms circled his neck, her muscles taut as piano wire, her body pressing against him, seeking his warmth, her senses flaring as she made contact with his warm, virile hardness, her heart sobbing within her with pain and pleasure.

'Oh, Falco!' Did she say it, or was it only in her head? It issued from her like a cry of desperation. A desperation born of a sudden aching need that she had stifled for so long and could no longer contain.

His lips pressed against hers, burning, consuming, as though the hunger in him was as immense as her own.

'Now do you remember?' His voice was harsh with passion. 'Now do you remember what it was like?'

'I had never forgotten. How on earth could I?'

Once again she was unsure whether she had said it or simply thought it. Her fingers were in his hair, smoothing, caressing, then sliding down to his shoulders to embrace the hard muscles. And every inch of him that she touched was a delight rediscovered. A flight back into the past. She knew this body so well.

And Falco had not forgotten either, as he proceeded to demonstrate. He still knew how to make her senses sing with pleasure.

As his lips consumed her, drawing the breath from her body, as they rained kisses of molten fire across her face, scorching her chin, her cheek, her temple, making her shiver with luscious pleasure as they found the hollow of her neck, his hands were working their own subtle magic.

Her blouse slid easily from the waistband of her skirt. The buttons fell open without any effort at all. And then, there she was, exposed and vulnerable, only the thin wisp of lace that was her bra to protect her from his unstoppable attentions.

But she had no wish to stop him, as, with a delicate impatience, he slipped the bra straps from her shoulders, loosening the cups that held her firm. Then with one sensuous movement he slid both hands inside to take simultaneous possession of each eager upturned breast.

'This is what you like...'

His palms grazed her hardening nipples and Laura felt her body buckle with helpless pleasure. 'Oh, yes!' she murmured, thrusting against him. Her breath felt as rough as gravel in her throat.

He continued to caress her, squeezing, his hands circling, the pleasure he inflicted a kind of torture. I shall die, Laura was thinking, if he should stop.

And her own hands, all the while, were growing ever bolder, unbuttoning his shirt to expose his dark-tanned chest, moulding the hard muscles, sliding down across his belly. The way his breath caught as she caressed him made her stomach turn to water.

It felt so natural, so easy to be like this with him again, as natural and easy as walking and breathing. That earlier sense of horror and incredulity had quite fled. All that was left was an all-consuming yearning—and that no more bitter-sweet, but as toothsome as honey.

And he felt the same way. Her spirit sensed it.

At least until he shattered her illusion.

All at once, his hands and his lips had grown still. He drew back a little from her. He looked into her face. And the expression in his eyes was as cold as marble.

'Not bad,' he smiled, 'considering you did it for nothing.' His lips twisted as the blood ebbed and flowed in her face, finally leaving her cheeks as pale as parchment. 'Just think what you might be prepared to offer me were I to name an acceptable price.'

Laura could not speak. Her limbs had turned to lead. A wave of engulfing nausea possessed her.

She tore her eyes from Falco's and fumbled with her blouse buttons, as with a contemptuous little movement he stepped away from her and observed,

'Shall we continue with our tour? I believe that was the purpose of our encounter.'

Then he was turning away from her and heading for the door, leaving Laura where she stood, unable to move, her body limp, her soul sinking in a sea of boiling shame.

CHAPTER SIX

THE rest of Falco's and Laura's tour of the villa was conducted in virtually total frosty silence. The few words that passed between them were stiff and formal, and rationed to only what was strictly essential. Not once was there even a flicker of eye contact between them.

But now at last the tour was over.

'I think we've covered everything.' They were standing in the drawing-room, at opposite ends of the big bay window. 'Unless,' Falco added, 'there's anything else you'd like me to show you?'

The twist of mocking humour in his tone had not eluded her. Without even a glance at him, her gaze fixed beyond the window, Laura answered spikily, 'No, thank you. I think we've covered everything.'

She was finding his attitude increasingly unbearable. Plain hostility she could have coped with, but the contemptuous amusement that surfaced now and then from beneath the hostility made her want to scratch his eyes out.

Why had he drawn her into that amorous embrace if his sole intention had been to make a fool of her? Had it simply been an exercise to test the extent of the power that he still mistakenly believed he wielded over her? Had his intention been to humiliate her? Did that kind of thing amuse him?

She continued to glare out of the window as he spoke now. 'Would you care for something to drink? I think I'll have a beer. Come and join me out on the terrace.'

Laura half turned then to look at him, her blue eyes narrowing. Go drown in your beer, she thought to herself spitefully. Aloud, she answered, 'If you don't mind, I'd rather not. I think I'll go to my room now. I have a bit of a headache.'

One black eyebrow lifted in a show of mocking sympathy. 'A headache? How unfortunate. Speak to Anna—I'm sure she'll be able to give you something for it.'

Laura ignored his solicitation. 'It seems to be catching. Headaches, I mean. A female hazard in this household. I wonder if it has anything to do with the male company?'

'Me, you mean?'

'Are there any other men here?'

'Not that I'm aware of.' He smiled at her insolently and leaned casually against the back of one of the sofas. 'But, personally, I would say that your particular headache has less to do with me and more to do with yourself.'

'Meaning?'

He held her eyes. 'I think you know what I mean.'

Laura glanced away, discomfited by that taunt. She sensed that what he meant were things she'd rather not dwell on.

Then she swept her gaze up again and accused him angrily, '*You're* the one who ought to be feeling bad. *You're* the one with a girlfriend not a million miles away from here!'

Her accusation had all the impact of a ton of feathers. Falco shrugged. 'I can see no point in feeling bad. You, it would appear, are feeling bad enough for both of us.'

'And I'm also the one who has no reason to feel so.' She tossed her head at him. 'I'm a free agent. I wasn't being unfaithful to anyone.'

As she said it, Laura realised that it was perfectly true. She had no reason at all to feel bad—apart, of course, from the unfortunate fact that she'd allowed Falco to get close enough to make her look an idiot. The way she had reacted to his kisses, though regrettable, had at least been healthy and honest. It was *his* behaviour that did not bear close scrutiny.

But he was as impervious as she had expected him to be to her insinuations. He simply leaned more comfortably against the back of the sofa and eyed her curiously. 'Is that so? There's no boyfriend back home waiting impatiently for your return?'

'That's more or less what I just told you.'

His eyes narrowed as he looked at her. 'Not even some sharp-suited antiques dealer? That used to be your preference, did it not?'

Had she been less flustered it might have crossed Laura's mind to wonder how Falco came to know the man had been an antiques dealer. She, for sure, had never told him.

But that detail escaped her. She felt a knife cut inside her, as she always did when he made those accusations. But this time she felt no desire to blurt out the truth. A most desirable development, she reflected as she hit back at him,

GET 4 BOOKS
A CUDDLY TEDDY
AND A MYSTERY GIFT

FREE

Return this card, and we'll send you 4 Mills & Boon Romances, absolutely FREE! We'll even pay the postage and packing for you!

We're making you this offer to introduce you to the benefits of Mills & Boon Reader Service: free home delivery of brand-new Romance novels, at least a month before they're available in the shops, FREE gifts and a monthly Newsletter packed with offers and information.

Accepting these 4 free books places you under no obligation to buy, you may cancel at any time, even just after receiving your free shipment.

Yes, please send me 4 free Mills & Boon Romances, a Cuddly Teddy and a Mystery Gift as explained above. Please also reserve a Reader Service Subscription for me. If I decide to subscribe, I shall receive six superb new titles every month for just £10.20 postage & packing free. If I decide not to subscribe I shall write to you within 10 days. The free books and gifts will be mine to keep in any case. I understand that I am under no obligation whatsoever. I may cancel or suspend my subscription at any time simply by writing to you.

Ms/Mrs/Miss/Mr ——————————————— 4A3R

Address ————————————————————

————————————————— Postcode—————————

Signature———————————————————————
I am over 18 years of age.

Get 4 Books
a Cuddly Teddy and
Mystery Gift FREE!

SEE BACK OF CARD FOR DETAILS

Mills & Boon Reader Service,
FREEPOST
P.O. Box 236
Croydon
CR9 9EL

Offer expires 31st August 1993. One per household. The right is reserved to refuse an application and change the terms of this offer. Offer applies to U.K. and Eire only. Readers overseas please send for details. Southern Africa write to: Book Services International Ltd., P.O. Box 41654 Craighall, Transvaal 2024. You may be mailed with offers from other reputable companies as a result of this application.

If you would prefer not to share these opportunities, please tick this box. ☐

mps
MAILING
PREFERENCE
SERVICE

'At the time he was an improvement on what I'd been used to. My previous romantic experiences had been of a pretty low standard.'

'Is that so?' His tone gave nothing away, but Laura had caught a tell-tale flicker at the back of his eyes.

She had got to him, she realised, astonished, triumphant, yet suddenly, inexplicably, overcome by a longing to apologise and take the insult back. However much she hated him, it still seemed a travesty to denigrate what had been the greatest romantic experience of her life.

Still, she was glad she had kept her apologies to herself as he proceeded to respond with an insult of his own. 'Well, at the rate you go through men—off with the old and on with the new before the sheets have time to grow cold—no doubt by now you've managed to put your early bad experiences behind you.'

'At least I dump the old one before taking on the new one—which is rather more than can be said for you. You don't even have the decency to be faithful to your girlfriend while she's living under your roof!'

Falco straightened slightly, the dark eyes evasive. 'Maybe you're right. But you can hardly talk. I wasn't aware of any overwhelming sense of decency emanating from you upstairs in the library. If I wronged Janine, you were a part of it, too.'

Laura could not deny that. She let her eyes glide away. Upstairs in the library the wrong she was doing Janine had never even entered her head.

Then she turned away sharply. She'd had enough of this discussion. All it was doing was making her headache worse.

'I'm going upstairs.' She strode across the room, heading for the door that led out into the hallway. 'If you don't mind, I'm going to lie down for a while.'

'Be my guest.' His tone was mocking. 'Feel free to lie down for as long as you like. Though I suspect that lying down in a darkened room isn't going to cure your sort of headache. What you need is an altogether different remedy.'

Laura was halfway through the door, deliberately ignoring him, when he added, 'Oh, by the way, when you've had your little rest perhaps you'd be good enough to answer me one question . . .'

There was something in his tone that caused Laura to turn and look at him.

And she could already feel her blood turn to ice as he held her eyes for an endless moment and demanded with just the hint of a demonic little smile,

'What I'd like you to tell me is . . . who is Belle?'

How Laura made it to her room she would never know. Her feet—her whole body—felt like lumps of dead wood. From head to toe she felt numb with horror.

She lay down on the bed, her heart pounding inside her. How had he found out? Had he known all along? Should she cut and run now? What would become of her?

But, gradually, the blur of fear in her head subsided. As she lay there on the silk bedspread, breathing slowly, her thinking was becoming sharper, more clearly focused.

Perhaps he didn't know anything, apart from Belle's name—though how he had come to discover that she could not begin to imagine. But she would be foolish to panic. That would serve no purpose. She must brazen this out. She must keep a tight grip on herself.

She rose from the bed and walked stiffly to the bathroom, dived under the shower, as cold as she could bear it, then briskly rubbed herself down with a towel. She would cope with this new nightmare. Somehow. And overcome it.

It was only as she was combing the wet tangles from her hair, reflecting that at least this new shock had cured her headache, that she suddenly paused and glanced at her reflection in the big silver-framed mirror over the wash basin. And as she looked at herself, a shudder went through her. What on earth had possessed her earlier in the library?

She dropped her gaze away. The answer was easy. All that was required was that she be honest. What had possessed her had been raw undiluted passion, the like of which she hadn't experienced for years.

For three years, to be precise. The last time she had felt such yearning had been the last time she had surrendered herself to Falco's embrace.

She remembered the occasion as though it were yesterday. They had been together at his flat in Solihull on the evening before he flew off to Belgium.

'I can't bear the thought of leaving you,' he had told her, kissing her and hugging her so fiercely that it was almost as though some sixth sense was warning him this was the last time together they would have.

Laura, too, had felt distressed, just as she always did whenever he had to go on off on these business trips for his father. She had buried her face against him. 'It's going to be awful without you. Promise me you'll think of me every single day.'

'Every minute of every single day.' His lips were in her hair, his hands caressing her, holding her against him, as though he would never let her go. 'Don't you know how much I love you?'

She'd smiled, foolishly confident in spite of her sadness. 'I think you love me almost as much as I love you.'

'More!' he'd protested, just as he always did.

'Impossible!' she'd countered, hugging him, adoring him. 'No one could possibly love anyone more than I love you!'

As she remembered that night, a lump rose to Laura's throat. Little had she known then, as they had lain together, making passionate love amid the tangle of bedclothes, that this was their swansong, the final act of their love-affair. And that the love she had seemed to see shining from his eyes was destined soon to turn to hate.

She swallowed hard. There had been no one else since. No one she had loved the way she had loved Falco. Falco and love—particularly the physical side of love—had remained inextricably, if illogically, bound together in her consciousness.

And that was why what had happened in the library had happened. When he had kissed her she had been transported back into the past, a past that was the only experience of love she had. It was as though the past and the present had suddenly become one.

Laura took a deep breath and laid aside her hair-brush, aware that her heart was thundering inside her. She should not think of these things, but she could not help it. Suddenly they filled her to overflowing.

She looked into her heart and found her thoughts focusing on that letter she had sent him eighteen months ago. She had told herself she had written it out of a sense of duty, believing he had a right to know about his daughter. And there was truth in that. But not the whole truth.

It was only when, two weeks later, she'd received Falco's curt reply, informing her that they had nothing to discuss, that, devastated, she'd been forced to face the truth.

Up until that moment, she had suddenly realised, the hope of seeing him again had filled her with new life. The hope of seeing him and the hope of what might come of their meeting. For she had planned not only to tell him about Belle, but also to explain what had really happened, how she was not to blame for their tragic parting.

Then he would forgive her and she would forgive him. And there would be nothing in the world to stop them being together again.

It was only when these hopes had fallen apart in her hands that she'd realised just how terrifyingly much they'd meant to her. And the realisation had deeply shocked her. It had almost driven her to the floor with shame.

How could she still feel this way for a man who, in the end, had proved to have so little faith in her?

Since the break-up she'd been telling herself that she hated him, that she wished never to set eyes on him as long as she lived.

And she had acted as though it were so. She'd built a whole new life for herself, a life that centred round her precious little daughter. She had managed perfectly without him.

She walked back into the bedroom and sat on the bed. Though she had scorned his arrogant claim that the sole purpose of the letter had been to beg his forgiveness and seek a reconciliation, he had not been so terribly wide of the mark. But, in spite of what had happened in the library, he was wrong if he believed that she still felt that way.

Her lapse in the library had been a reflex action, an involuntary response to the tug of old sexual strings that ought to have been severed a long time ago. Well, they were severed now. It would never happen again. If he ever made another move in her direction, he would soon find that out. She would not stand for it.

Angrily, she clenched her fists, remembering how he had humiliated her. Had that all been part of some sadistic little build-up, a callous, deliberate bid to demoralise her before he dropped his final bombshell?

Laura felt her heart stand still, remembering the insolent way he had asked the question that had caused the blood to freeze. 'What I'd like you to tell me is...who is Belle?'

With a wrenching sigh, she covered her face with her hands, as all the old fears rose up again inside her. He had already, three years ago, come close to destroying her. He would not do it a second time. He would never take Belle from her.

She stood up abruptly, suddenly unable to bear all the pain and anger and fear and confusion that swarmed like fork-tongued serpents inside her. This man whom she had once loved and who had so callously betrayed her, this man who could still scorch her soul with his kisses, this man who was the father of her little daughter... she would fight him with every weapon she could lay her hands on.

A tear spilled down her cheek. Despite her iron resolution, her heart was suddenly the saddest, most desolate spot on earth.

What Laura had been fearing all day had not happened.

From the moment she'd finally emerged from her room, her spirit steeled for confrontation, she'd been waiting for Falco to appear suddenly before her and demand an answer to his question: who is Belle?

But though their paths had crossed briefly on several occasions, to her surprise and relief no such thing had happened. It was as though he had forgotten, or lost interest in the matter. It was as though he had never even asked the awful question.

Laura decided to regard this as a favourable sign. For she felt certain that if he'd already known who Belle was, or even if he'd only suspected the truth, he'd have wasted no time in pinning her down.

Yet, though she felt deeply soothed by the logic of that assumption, her heart still lay unquiet within her. By what devious means had he come to know there was someone called Belle in her life?

She was still asking herself that question as she got ready for dinner, brushing her hair into its customary neat blonde bob and slicking mascara on to her lashes. Perhaps she would never have the answer. And perhaps—she crossed her fingers—it didn't matter. Perhaps the subject had been dropped.

Perhaps. She frowned at her reflection in the mirror. But don't count on it, she warned herself.

There was no outward sign of her inner anxiety as Laura swept into the drawing-room just before eight, dressed in a cheerful peacock-blue dress that left one shoulder bare and was tied in a knot over the other. She was becoming an expert, she thought wryly, at disguising her fears.

Falco and Janine were sitting out on the patio enjoying an aperitif before dinner. Following the sound of their voices, Laura joined them.

She smiled a greeting. 'I hope I haven't kept you waiting?'

'Not at all.' Falco swivelled round to face her. He was dressed in a stone-coloured silk and linen suit, a rusty-red silk tie at his throat. He looked, as ever, quite irritatingly handsome.

'Good.' Laura snatched her eyes away from his and turned her attention on Janine. 'I'm glad to see you'll be joining us this evening.'

That was straight from the heart. Any confrontation with Falco was unlikely to take place when Janine was present. Knowing that, Laura felt her inner anxiousness dissolve and a sense of buoyant relief take its place.

Janine, looking pretty in a peach-coloured dress, was smiling at her, as she replied, 'Me, too. It'll give us a chance to get to know each other. We haven't had much of a chance to talk so far.' She cast a coy glance in Falco's direction. 'According to Falco, you're a very interesting lady.'

Well, how about that? Laura suppressed a wry smile and wondered just how interesting she was supposed to be. Did this mean Falco had told Janine about their past?

That was doubtful, she decided, as she answered, smiling, 'I'm sure that's just Falco's naturally generous nature. He seems always to be saying complimentary things about people.'

The irony in the remark eluded Janine entirely. She smiled again, that coy innocent smile of hers, leaned towards Falco and playfully tweaked his cheek. 'Yes, he is a bit of a sweetie, isn't he?' she cooed. 'Positively the sweetest man I've ever known.'

'Me too. I'm forever thinking that. Falco Roth is the sweetest man on earth.'

Laura managed to keep her face straight as she said it. I should be in movies, she was thinking to herself. That was worthy of an Oscar.

Falco evidently thought so too. The black eyes that looked back at her were filled with wicked complimentary amusement. He said, laying a counter-claim to her imaginary Oscar, 'But then people like you make it easy to be kind. How could any man fail to be generous with his praises when it comes to an enchanting young woman like yourself?'

Janine laughed, delighted. 'You have such a way with words!' She leaned towards him and hugged his arm affectionately. 'I've never known a man like you!'

That was undoubtedly more accurate than the poor girl realised, Laura thought to herself as she watched the little scene. And again she felt a stab of compassion for Janine. She seemed so smitten with Falco and so secure in their relationship—not a flicker of jealousy had touched those trusting grey eyes—that it seemed almost a sin to stand passively by and not warn her of the terrible danger she was in.

This man whom she believed to be the essence of sweetness one day would turn on her with the poisonous fangs of a viper.

For the moment, however, he was merely rising to his feet, a polite smile on his lips, to offer Laura a drink.

'Campari?' he enquired. 'Since you're off your usual.'

'Campari would be lovely.'

'With ice and lemon?'

Laura nodded. 'Yes, thank you.' And inwardly she scowled. That reference to her 'usual' was a small betrayal of Janine. It was a deliberate reference to a part of his past to which his girlfriend, she was still certain, had not been made privy. It was a fine example of his deceit and insensitivity.

Poor Janine, she thought again. She's heading for heartbreak.

Yet she could be wrong, Laura found herself reflecting, as later they sat around the table over dinner. Falco never quite managed to give the impression, as Janine did, that he was part of a couple. Yet there were moments when it was impossible not to be aware of the tenderness he quite evidently felt for the girl.

His eyes would swivel to look at her while her attention was elsewhere and a tiny concerned frown would crease his brow. He had the look then, unashamedly protective and caring, of a parent watching over a child.

Perhaps she had misjudged him a little over Janine, Laura found herself speculating in an ambivalent sort of way. For she was wondering too, though she crushed the thought instantly, if he had ever in the past looked at her the same way.

The conversation between the three of them flowed surprisingly easily, as easily as the wine that washed down the meal—mouth-watering and abundant—that Anna set before them.

'I'm going to burst!' Janine sat back, laughing, after their dessert plates had been cleared away. 'I've never eaten so much in my life!'

'Me, too. That was extraordinary!' Laura tossed down her napkin. She felt relaxed and easy. It had been an unexpectedly pleasant evening. 'I don't think I've ever tasted cooking like Anna's!' She glanced across at Falco, with whom, it occurred to her, for once she had not exchanged a single sharp word. 'Where did you find her? Did she come with the house?'

'More or less. Except she was planning to leave. She and her husband were going to move back to the mainland. But after I'd tasted her *tortellini al ragù* I was prepared to pay any amount to persuade her to stay on.'

'I can't say I blame you. Though you'd better beware.' Laura frowned across at him, mock serious. 'You'll be turning into a Pavarotti if you eat like this every day!'

'Oh, Falco's lucky. He doesn't have that problem.' Janine chipped in instantly to put her right. 'He can eat as much as he wants and he doesn't put on an ounce.'

Yes, I remember. Laura very nearly said it. But she checked herself in time, though the thought had discomfited her. Just for an instant she'd been swept back into the past again. The past that seemed constantly to keep drawing her into its clutches.

With a conscious effort she tugged herself back to the present, leaning back in her chair and glancing round the room. 'You know, this is a potentially splendid room. Perfect proportions. I'm going to really enjoy doing it.'

'So you've been thinking shop while we've been eating?' Falco glanced across at her with a curious smile. 'Have you come up with any good ideas?'

'One or two.'

He smiled. 'Including that rectangular table?'

'Oh, yes. The rectangular table is absolutely essential.'

Laura said it as though she meant it, though it had actually struck her on more than one occasion in the course of the evening that a more democratic round table would have suited the evening's mood better.

A one-off, she reproached herself. This evening's charming façade, she of all people ought to know was just that—a façade. Behind it lay all the Roth ruthlessness of his loathsome father.

It also struck her that they were having another private conversation, full of allusions to which Janine was not privy. That made her feel guilty. She was colluding in his insensitivity.

Very deliberately, she turned to Janine. 'How would you like to see this room,' she asked her, 'if you were in charge of its decoration?'

'Me?' Janine's pencilled eyebrows lifted. 'Don't ask me. I'm no good at things like that. I don't have any of your talents. I'm just a secretary.'

'A damned good secretary.' Falco cut in at once. And there it was again, that look on his face, that look of almost parental protectiveness. His hand was on Janine's arm. 'Don't keep putting yourself down. You have plenty of talents, and don't you forget it.'

It was touching the way he had rushed to her defence, for there had been a sad hint of self-deprecation in Janine's remark. And his support had quite plainly done wonders for her ego. She was quite literally smiling from ear to ear as she blew him a kiss across the table.

'OK. If you say so, Falco,' she giggled.

Laura sat back in her seat, oddly baffled. His attitude to Janine was so full of contradictions. Almost indifferent at times, excluding her from conversations, then suddenly so full of kindness that it caught at one's throat.

He was a puzzle, she decided. But not her puzzle. Poor smitten Janine was more than welcome to him.

Anna arrived at that moment with a tray of coffee things and a message.

'There's someone on the phone,' she told Falco in her broken English. 'I'm sorry I couldn't make out who it was.'

'Don't worry. I'll see to it.' Falco rose to his feet. Then before leaving the room, he addressed Laura and Janine. 'I've asked Anna to serve coffee out on the patio. You make yourselves comfortable. I'll be with you in a minute.'

'Isn't he wonderful?' As the two girls rose from their chairs, Janine grinned with starry eyes at Laura. 'Isn't he just the most wonderful man you could imagine?'

Laura smiled as best she could. 'He has his moments.' She picked up her still half-full glass of red wine and headed with Janine out on to the patio, where Anna was arranging the coffee things on one of the white-painted iron tables. Then, suddenly curious, she added, 'How long have you known Falco?'

'A couple of months or so.' Janine giggled. 'Not so long.' Then her expression became earnest. 'But he's completely changed my life. Getting to know Falco was the best thing that ever happened to me.'

'That's quite a claim to make.'

'I know, and I mean it. Falco turned my whole world around.'

Laura hesitated, wondering if she should make some cautionary comment. The girl's devotion to Falco was downright dangerous. But before she could decide, Falco appeared in the doorway.

'Janine,' he was saying, 'it's for you.'

As he stood there, beckoning to her, Janine was hurrying towards him. Then as she approached him, he caught her arm and whispered something in her ear, some endearment, by the looks of things, that caused her to grin broadly, fling her arms around his neck and kiss him warmly before hurrying off to take her phone call.

Love's young dream, Laura thought cynically, taking a sip of her wine.

Falco, she sensed, was unaware that she had been watching them. She had been half turned away, but she turned to face him now, as he stepped out on to the patio, his hands in his trouser pockets, his step light, with his usual air of self-assurance.

'Thank you,' he was saying to Anna, as the woman hurried back indoors. Then to Laura he observed, coming to stand right in front of her, 'I haven't had an opportunity to compliment you before, but you're looking, if I may say so, particularly stunning this evening.'

'Am I?' Laura's tone was not overflowing with approval. He hadn't had an opportunity to compliment her, she was thinking, because his girlfriend had been at his side the entire evening.

He held her eyes. 'Yes, that colour suits you. I always did rather like you in blue.'

Laura felt anger rise inside her at this shameless come-on. 'If I'd remembered,' she answered crisply, 'I'd have worn red instead.'

To her annoyance, he simply smiled and continued to hold her eyes. Then he shifted slightly. The dark eyes narrowed. 'You know, you still haven't answered my question.'

Just for an instant, quite genuinely, she was baffled. Laura frowned. 'What question haven't I answered?'

His eyes held hers. 'The one I asked you earlier.' He paused a beat. 'Tell me now. Who is Belle?'

Bafflement, in an instant, was replaced by blinding panic. Laura froze to the spot. 'No one,' she croaked.

'She can't be no one.' The dark eyes were still on her, their expression remote, oddly unreadable. 'I heard you talking about her on the phone.'

So, that was how he came to know about Belle! 'You've been listening in to my phone conversations!' In defence, Laura leapt straight into the attack. 'What a cheap thing to do! Have you no shame?'

'It was quite unintentional.' He remained calm against her onslaught. 'The lines sometimes get crossed, and that's what must have happened the other day when I picked up my own phone to make a call. I didn't overhear much—I laid the receiver down immediately—but I did just catch you saying, "How's Belle? Is she well?"'

He paused, the dark eyes seeming to pierce through her. 'There was such a note of concern in your voice that I couldn't help wondering who Belle was.'

'No one. I told you. No one that need concern you.' Her tone was rough in spite of the relief that poured through her. She'd been right, he hadn't a clue who Belle was—not even that she was her daughter and certainly not that she was his! He was simply prying into her privacy in an effort to discomfit her.

She repeated, 'Who she is is no business of yours.'

He was still watching her. 'No need to get so upset about it.' He smiled. 'It was just an innocent question.' And then, suddenly, he was doing the unforgivable. He was reaching out to touch her arm.

It was the shock of the sudden heat of his hand, causing her skin to prickle and her heart to jump wildly, that seemed to trigger an unstoppable explosion within her.

Laura snatched her arm away and glared at him in fury. 'Don't you have any shame at all laying hands on another woman the minute your girlfriend's out of sight?' She gulped a furious breath. 'If only you knew how I despise you!'

Then, to her own astonishment as much as his, she was flinging the contents of her wine glass in his face, slamming the empty glass down on the table and storming back into the house, overcome with emotion, yet no longer quite certain what it was she was fleeing from.

CHAPTER SEVEN

AFTER that histrionic outburst on the patio, Laura decided to steer clear of Falco for a while.

Over the next few days, when she wasn't roaming the house, making copious sketches and jotting down ideas, or going for rides on the bike Falco had said she could borrow, she would spend a relaxing hour down on the beach with Janine, or join the other girl for a cool drink on the terrace.

And, almost always when she sought her out, Janine was available. Available and alone. Falco was scarcely ever with her.

'Isn't he neglecting you a bit?' she enquired lightheartedly, as they flopped down on to their beach towels after a swim one afternoon. She had no wish to upset Janine or make her feel insecure, but almost the only time they ever saw Falco these days was at mealtimes.

But Janine seemed unconcerned. 'Oh, he has things to do.' With a serene smile, she proceeded to rub sun oil over her arms.

'Couldn't he take you with him?' If he was *my* boyfriend, Laura was thinking, I wouldn't be so understanding about being left alone so much of the time.

Janine shook her head. 'It's business, mostly. If he took me along, I'd only get in the way.' Then she turned those innocent grey eyes on her inquisitor. 'Falco knows what's best. And I could never accuse him of neglecting me. He's wonderful to me. I adore him. I really do.'

There was no answer to that. Laura shrugged and changed the subject. But again she felt that dart of worry. Janine really was in serious danger.

'I thought you were going to stay down there forever. I was wondering if I ought to dive in and fish you out.'

'How very gallant.' Laura shook her dripping head and removed the snorkel mouthpiece from her mouth. She regarded Falco with sharp displeasure through the window of her diving mask, her eyes flicking to check if Janine was with him. But he was alone, alas. Laura instantly smelled trouble.

She remained where she was, bobbing in the aquamarine water while Falco sat watching her from his perch on the rock.

'I was passing,' he observed, 'and I spotted your bicycle. And then I noticed your clothes and things on the rock. I thought I'd stick around and find out what you were up to.'

Passing, indeed! More likely he had come looking for her with the precise intention of spoiling her day. This rocky little corner was miles away from the villa, literally on the opposite side of the island. It had taken her the best part of an hour to cycle here.

Laura told him, 'What I've been up to is gathering some shells from the seabed.' So saying, she paddled up to the edge of the rock face and deposited her latest handful of booty alongside her earlier acquisitions in a narrow dip on a small jutting ledge.

She was careful, as she did so, to avoid brushing Falco's foot which was placed, brown and sinuous, just an inch or two away.

'Very pretty.' He leaned across to cast a glance at her collection. 'Any particular reason for collecting them?'

'As a matter of fact, there is.'

Laura could sense that she was scowling as she looked up at him through the window of her mask. He was sitting there, dressed in white T-shirt and trousers, knowing perfectly well just how much his presence irked her, and, to judge from his expression, thoroughly enjoying her annoyance. She felt like telling him to get lost, but that would be a little inappropriate. This was his island and his rock. He had every right to be here!

'Are you going to tell me what it is, this reason for your endeavours? Or do I have to guess?' He smiled as he said it. Yes, he was enjoying this situation hugely.

Laura shrugged her shoulders, which were still the only part of her that she had allowed to emerge from the lapping blue sea. 'I'll tell you. It's no secret. It's an idea I've had, to construct a kind of mosaic of coral and seashells in the hallway of the villa.'

Falco seemed to think a moment. 'That could be quite striking.'

'I thought it would be appropriate, particularly in the entrance hall. A kind of marrying of the interior with the outside environment.'

'I like the idea.'

'I'm not sure if it'll work.' Thanks to his approval, Laura could feel herself starting to go off the idea.

'We'll just have to try it and see.'

'Yes, that was my intention.' His use of the word 'we' had caused her to stress the singular 'my'. It was childish, she knew, but that was the way he affected her.

There was a silence. Laura continued to bob in the water. Falco leaned back against the rock, observing her through his lashes. 'Pay no attention to me. Just carry on with what you were doing.'

But how could she, knowing that every time she surfaced she'd find him hovering over her like a vulture? She pushed back her mask to the top of her head. There had to be some way of getting rid of him.

'I'm just wondering why you're here. If you'd like to tell me what you want, we can sort that out, then each of us can get on with his own business.'

'I told you I was just passing.'

'And decided to stop for a chat? Well, I'm busy, as you can see. I don't have time for chatting.'

'Then I'll just sit here and watch you. It's all the same to me. That is, unless you have any objections?'

Laura took a deep breath, counted slowly to ten and searched within herself for restraint.

She said, calmly, 'It seems like rather a waste of your time.'

'It's my time to waste.' He stretched out his long legs and leaned back more comfortably, as though he was planning on a long vigil. 'Besides, it's quite a while since I had you all to myself.'

Laura bobbed impatiently. 'That must be breaking your heart.'

'You seem to be spending all of your time with Janine these days.'

'Only when I'm not working.'

'You've developed quite a little sisterhood.' He emphasiscd that last word with scathing amusement.

Laura ignored his sarcasm. 'She's the only one who's ever here.'

'Even at mealtimes you huddle beside her. I've started to get the impression that you're trying to avoid me.'

Laura frowned for a moment, rejecting his accusation. She preferred to sit with Janine, but she certainly didn't huddle!

He'd got it right, though, with his suggestion that she'd been trying to avoid him. She said, 'Is there any reason you can think of why I should want to seek out your company?'

'To apologise perhaps.'

'Apologise for what?'

'For ruining a shirt and one of my favourite silk ties.'

Laura blushed to her hairline, yet she felt reluctant to apologise. Such histrionic gestures as throwing wine in people's faces were not normally her style, but he had deserved it. That shameless pass, the moment Janine was out of sight, had been precisely the sort of behaviour she had decided she would not stand for.

'Are they really ruined?' was all she said.

'Red wine is notoriously difficult to shift.' He regarded her for a moment, then he observed, 'So, you really do feel strongly about such things?'

'About infidelity, you mean?'

He nodded. 'Precisely.'

'Yes. I feel very strongly indeed.'

There was another short pause, then he laughed ironically. 'Funny,' he said, 'you could have fooled me.'

'And what is that supposed to mean?' She felt another blush rise up. He was about to allude to that episode in the library.

But he proceeded to cast her mind further back than that. 'It means that, as I have pointed out to you before, once upon a time you were not so fastidious. Three years ago you were off like a shot with another man almost as soon as I was out of your sight.' His eyes bored into her, accusing and unforgiving. 'So don't try and tell me about all your high moral principles!'

Laura felt her stomach heave. He made her sound like filth. And he hadn't finished with her yet. Harsh-faced, he went on to accuse her, 'And don't waste your time telling me how much you despise me! You don't even know what the word "despise" means. But I do. You taught me. When you took my father's money. I never knew I could despise anyone the way I despised you for that.'

Laura half wished she could just sink into the sea and drown. Anything to escape that look on his face. She closed her eyes, her cheeks suddenly cold and ashen. Her lips fell open, silently pleading with him to stop.

But he did not stop. 'How does it feel?' he demanded, his anger and his hatred of her leaping from every pore. 'How does it feel to live your life knowing you're the kind of person who'll do absolutely anything for money?'

She could not listen to him. Laura began to paddle backwards, away from him, out to sea, her eyes burning with tears.

'How can you bear to look at yourself in the mirror?' He had risen to his feet now and was shouting after her. 'How can you do it? Doesn't it make you sick?'

Frantically, Laura paddled, covering her ears with her hands. But his words still reached her, tainting her with their poison.

Then, suddenly something snapped inside her.

Laura took a deep breath and flung the words at him. 'I didn't take the money! Not a damned penny! Not a damned penny! Do you hear?'

Then she was swinging away, flinging herself into the waves, striking out towards the horizon like a woman possessed. Tears were pouring from her eyes, hot and salty, mingling with the cold salt of the sea.

She would have swum forever. Until her body was exhausted. Until she was incapable of swimming another single stroke.

But all at once, against her will, she was being dragged to a halt, her body hauled round to face a pair of blazing black eyes.

'What did you say?' Falco was demanding, holding her as tightly as the tentacles of an octopus.

She could not speak for sobbing. He shook her again, violently.

'What did you say? That you didn't take the money?'

Laura shook her head helplessly. She felt numb with misery. 'Not a single penny! I wouldn't have touched it. I wouldn't have touched your father's filthy money!'

Still he was holding her, the dark eyes boring into her. 'Do you mean that? Are you serious? Are you telling me the truth?'

'Why won't you believe me? What do you take me for?' Her voice caught in her throat. She choked on a sob. 'How could you, even for one minute, have believed such a thing of me?'

His arms were round her now, holding her, comforting her, drawing her against him with all the gentleness in the world.

'I believe you,' he told her, his voice thick with emotion. 'I believe you, Laura. I believe every word.'

'Truly?' She was looking up at him, her tear-streaked face puffy. Suddenly it was important to her that he was speaking the truth.

'Truly, my love. Truly.' He wiped the tears from her face, held her close for a moment and pressed his lips against her temple. 'And I've never been happier to be wrong in my life.'

Laura half smiled then. 'How very unlike you.' Suddenly she felt a sense of extraordinary lightness, as though an enormous weight had been lifted from her. And suddenly, too, she was acutely conscious of Falco's arms around her and of his hard male body beneath the trousers and T-shirt he still wore.

She laughed a nervous laugh. 'You dived in with all your clothes on!'

But he simply pulled her closer. 'Why didn't you tell me earlier? Why did I have to force it out of you? Is that what you were planning to tell me when you wrote me that letter?'

Laura felt her heart turn over with too many emotions. Part of her was suddenly longing to tell him everything, but she answered with a cautious half-truth. 'Yes.'

Falco drew a deep breath, as though this revelation pained him. He pulled her even more tightly against him. 'I'm sorry. Forgive me,' he murmured against her hair.

They were words she had never even dreamed of hearing. Unexpectedly, they filled her heart to overflowing.

With a sigh Laura wrapped her arms around his neck. 'Oh, Falco! Falco!' The whispered name was like a prayer.

'Laura . . . Dear Laura . . .' He drew back to gaze at her. 'I should have known. I should have known without you telling me that you could never have taken that money.'

'No, how could you?'

She shook her head and fell silent. Suddenly all the words in the world seemed superfluous. For in that moment as they bobbed in the limpid blue water, gazing at one another, bodies wrapped together, something seemed to pass between them that wiped the slate clean and surpassed the need for explanations.

And that was when, with a shudder of fierce emotion, Falco bent his head to hers and kissed her.

*   *   *

Later, to recall that magical moment was to feel knives twisting and turning inside her heart. Yet until the day she died, she was destined, Laura knew, to remember it in vivid, burning detail.

They had clung to one another like barnacles to a rock, their lips exchanging hot salty kisses, their bodies wrapped together, hungry for one another, laughing, almost weeping, lost in a storm of feeling, suddenly the only two people in the universe.

'This is crazy!' Falco said at last, hugging her hard against him. 'We're both going to drown if we keep this up!'

'I don't care!' Laura laughed, pressing her face against him. At least, she was thinking, I would die happy!

'Well, I care. Come on.' He wrapped his arms around her and drew her against him with her back against his front. Then he was paddling backwards towards the rocks, taking her with him, like a piggyback in reverse. 'I'm not going to lose you now,' he murmured against her hair.

The rock was warm as they scrambled from the water, the afternoon sun bright and hot against their backs. Laura flopped down on to the towel she had laid out on the rock earlier and lay watching, her heart filled with wonder and excitement, as Falco peeled off his wet things, right down to his blue swimming-trunks.

What a perfectly splendid specimen he was, with that lean, powerful physique of his! Those broad, muscular shoulders, mahogany-dark from the sun, that smooth rippling back, those long hard-packed legs. It made her shiver with pleasure just to look at him, and to imagine how that body felt when it was pressed against her own.

He had laid out his sopping T-shirt and trousers to dry and was turning now to look at her, a slight frown marring his smile.

'It's questions and answers time now,' he told her mock sternly, as he flopped down on the towel beside her and buried a kiss against her neck. 'And you don't get off this rock until I'm satisfied.'

Laura smiled back at him blissfully. She wanted to tell him everything, to make a clean breast, even to tell him about Belle. But I shall leave that revelation till the end, she decided. She would hand it to him like a gift once all the rest had been ironed out.

Falco was leaning over her, looking down into her face, the dark eyes with their thick silky fringe of black lashes full of earnest loving curiosity.

He pushed back a strand of wet hair from her face, kissing the place where it had been. 'So, you didn't walk out on me for money... We've established that.' He held his breath a moment. 'So, tell me, why did you?'

Laura looked into his face, feeling a sense of happy wonderment that the wall that had stood between them was about to be demolished. But, before answering him, she asked a question of her own.

'Why were you so certain I'd taken the money?'

Falco sighed and shook his head. 'My father showed me proof. He showed me a copy of the banker's draft he gave you.'

She had never thought of that. A frown creased Laura's brow. 'It's a pity he didn't also tell you that the draft in question was never cashed. I tore it up.

Right there in his office. I flung the pieces in his face.'

Laura had a moment's recollection of that bitter, heady moment when she had finally had her chance to express with that dramatic gesture the disgust and contempt she had always felt for Oscar Roth. How pleasing it had been to see his shocked expression. He had looked as though he longed to wring her neck.

'You mean he called you to his office and offered you money to break up with me?'

'Yes.'

'And you refused and tore up the banker's draft?'

Laura laughed a bitter laugh. 'Finally in his life he'd come up against someone who couldn't be bought. He couldn't believe it. I thought he was going to go crazy.'

Falco sighed. 'I can imagine.' Then he turned away a moment, tilted his head and gazed up at the sky.

Laura watched his dark profile. What was going through his head? Did he feel uncomfortable with her harsh words about his father?

Then he turned once more to look at her, the black eyes piercing through her. 'But you broke up with me anyway. Even without the money. Why? That's the question I really want answered.'

Laura took a deep breath. 'He made threats,' she told him.

Falco's body had stiffened. 'What kind of threats?'

'Threats against my father. He threatened to destroy him unless I broke off my relationship with you.'

'He what?' Falco looked back at her, astounded. 'Say that again. Explain precisely what you mean.'

Laura's heart had begun to flutter anxiously inside her. It had all happened three years ago, yet the agony had stayed with her. And she had never spoken of any of this to another living soul.

'It's very simple. Unless I broke off with you, your father threatened to fire my father—in spite of the fact that at that time he'd been with Roth Engineering for twenty-five years.'

Falco nodded. 'He's a first-class electrician, as I remember.'

'The best. Unfortunately, he also has a dicky heart—though that never stopped him doing his job—and he was over fifty when all of this happened.' She swallowed. These painful memories had made her throat dry. Then, as Falco continued to stroke her hair with his fingers, gently soothing her, she continued, 'And your father didn't simply threaten to fire him... He swore that he'd make sure my father never worked again.'

Falco's fingers grew still. A dark look touched his eyes. 'Are you serious? I can't believe this. What you're telling me is outrageous!'

'Outrageous, but true.' Her heart flickered within her. She had known he would find this part hard to swallow.

He had moved away with a sigh to lie on his back alongside her, staring at the sky. Laura could not see his eyes.

She continued, 'I knew he meant it. I knew I had to take it seriously. And I couldn't just stand by and watch my father thrown on to the scrap heap.

It would have killed him. He's a proud and decent man.'

There was a brief, deep silence, then Falco said quietly, 'Why didn't you tell me? Why didn't you tell me at the time?'

'I couldn't. If I told you, your father promised me he'd go ahead and fire my father anyway. It was a hopeless situation. My hands were completely tied. I had no choice but to comply with your father's wishes.'

'You should have told me!' He sounded angry. 'I still say you should have told me what the hell was going on!'

'And what could you have done?' Laura raised herself to look down at him. 'If you'd confronted your father, he would have known I'd told you and my father would have lost his job. There was nothing you could have done to prevent that. Your father was the boss. He could do anything he liked.'

Falco let out an oath and closed his eyes for a moment, breathing deeply and slowly to calm his boiling rage. Then he reached out and took hold of her, his fingers like vices.

'So, you just gave in and wrote me that letter and went off to London, turning your back on everything?'

He made it sound so easy. Like turning off a tap. If only he knew. The break had almost killed her.

She murmured, her heart twisting, 'I had no choice.'

He gazed into her face, the black eyes tormented. They seemed to bore right through to the back of her skull.

Then, with a wrenching sigh, he pulled her against him. 'You're right, you didn't. Of course you didn't,' he said.

For a long, emotional moment he held her against him, his arms tight around her, his hands caressing her back. Laura could feel the powerful beat of his heart.

Then he drew away a little, but still holding on to her, and with a frown looked down into her face.

'So, what changed? Something must have changed by the time you wrote me that letter. You wouldn't have written it if you'd still been afraid for your father's job.'

Laura nodded in agreement. 'Yes, things had changed by then. By then, my business was doing really well. I'd managed to save enough to lend my father enough money to allow him to set up in business on his own. It was what he'd always wanted, but it had never been possible. With his health record no bank would lend him the money.

'When I wrote you that letter, he'd already left Roth Engineering.' A frown touched her brow. Hadn't Falco even noticed that one of the company's senior electricians had gone? But for the moment at least she pushed that thought away. 'By then,' she continued, 'my father was safe from Oscar's threats. There was no longer any way your father could touch him.'

'That's quite a story. Quite a story. Now I understand the grudge you have against my father.'

Falco kissed her face as they lay very still together, only his hands moving as they softly stroked her hair, the only sound against the background splash of the sea the murmur of their breathing and the quiet beat of their hearts.

But though part of her, as they lay there together, embracing, was wishing that this moment might last forever, Laura was aware that one corner of her heart was drawing back. There was still so much she had been planning to tell him. Hadn't it been her intention, finally, to reveal all? Yet something, some instinct, was telling her to keep silent. Some inner voice was warning her to keep her secrets to herself.

Was it because of his careless revelation that he hadn't even noticed her father had left Roth Engineering? That unexpected and bitter reminder of how much he was still his father's son?

Perhaps. All she knew was that the wall that had stood between them had been only partially dismantled, and that was how it must remain.

She clung to him, trying to banish the feeling, for it chilled her heart. But she could not shake it off.

Then, at last, as the sun began to dip towards the horizon, Falco stirred. 'I think we should make a move now. Let's go back to the villa and have something to eat.'

Laura watched him as he got up and pulled on his trousers and T-shirt—now both quite dry, if somewhat in need of pressing!—and was aware of a forlorn tug at her heart. A short while ago, briefly, everything seemed to have changed. The sun had seemed to shine upon them. But really nothing had changed.

She pulled on her sundress over her swimsuit, gathered up her pile of shells and her sandals and followed Falco to where he had parked his car. He was stowing her bicycle in the boot when she caught up with him.

He turned suddenly to look at her, his dark eyes narrowed. 'There's just one thing. That flat you were living in... That sumptuous affair in the heart of St John's Wood... Since you didn't take my father's money, where on earth did you get the money to pay for it?'

Laura made a face. 'That's a very long story. Let me tell it to you some other time.'

Her heartbeat scurried as she said it. In fact, it was not such a very long story. She had ended up in that flat through a piece of simple good fortune. But that inner voice was still warning her to say no more.

Falco did not press her. He shrugged. 'OK. If you like, we can keep that one for another day.'

Then they were climbing into the car and heading back to the villa, Laura aware of a growing sense of discomfort, longing to be free of him, longing to be on her own, yet bewildered at the sudden intensity of this change in her.

As though to avoid conversation, she fiddled with her shells, laying them out in a handkerchief in her lap, without thinking what she was doing sorting them into piles.

I'm just tired, she told herself as she fiddled and sorted. It's been an intensely, highly emotional day. Perhaps I just need a little time to get used to all that's happened.

She was totally unaware that Falco was watching her, and when he spoke, his tone was so light and conversational that it barely jolted her out of her private reverie.

'What are all the little piles?' he asked her.

Laura answered without thinking, her mind only half on what she was saying. 'These are definitely for the mural. These are maybes.' She pointed idly with her finger. 'And these I'm going to take home to B——'

She felt like biting her tongue out. Her heart froze within her. She heard Falco say calmly,

'I think what you were about to say was Belle.' He paused. 'I take it this is the same Belle we talked about the other evening? The Belle you claimed was no one in particular?'

Laura could not look at him. Her hands lay stiffly in her lap now. The blood in her veins had turned to nails.

It was at that moment that they turned into the gateway of the villa and Laura was granted a brief reprieve. For, as they approached the front door, suddenly it was flung open and Janine, red hair flying, was rushing towards the car.

'Where have you been? I've been so worried!' she was calling.

And suddenly, through the paralysis that gripped her, Laura realised with a start that she had forgotten about Janine. This afternoon in the sea, lying with Falco on the rocks, she had entirely forgotten Janine's existence.

She understood now what the voice was that had been warning her to keep her secrets to herself. It had been her instinct for survival, her sense of decency, her conscience—call it what you will. Falco, in as much as he could belong to anyone, these days belonged to Janine.

Her heart was a lump of lead. But she had revealed her dearest secret, the one that mattered most to her to keep concealed. Falco was not a fool. He could put two and two together. He knew who Belle was now. He knew she was her daughter.

With painfully beating heart she turned to him quickly, before Janine could reach the car, and spoke in a rush the lie she knew she must tell him.

'You asked how I managed to pay for that flat... The one in St John's Wood... Well, it's really very simple. It belonged to my lover. That guy you saw me with. The antiques dealer with the gaudy tie and the Hitler moustache.'

She took a long shivering breath and forced herself to continue. 'And Belle, whom you're so curious about, is that man's daughter.'

Then she was climbing from the car and heading back to the villa, fists clenched tightly, her heart bursting inside her, feeling as though she were walking on shifting shale, sliding down into some bottomless black pit.

CHAPTER EIGHT

THANKS to that desperate, shocking lie Laura felt safe and protected once again.

For he had believed her. Falco had believed that the father of her child was that sleazy antiques dealer he had seen her with three years ago. A shutter had fallen at the back of his eyes. A look almost of pain had settled on his face. Not pain, she quickly corrected herself. More likely horrified distaste.

Well, she could understand that. Horrified distaste was more or less what the notion had stirred in her as well. But what choice had she had? He'd guessed that Belle was her daughter. And he must never be allowed to know that he was the father.

Laura stepped out on to the balcony of her room, dressed in a plain white cotton bathrobe, leaned against the railings and looked up at the sky. Perhaps, she was wondering, she had made, all for nothing, the sacrifice of staying on and accepting his commission. He now knew about Belle and it had been to keep that secret from him that she had forestalled his threatened trip to London.

But no, she decided, she'd been right to stay on here. That he now knew about Belle was quite bad enough, but if he'd gone to London and started mingling with her colleagues the outcome might well have been a full-blown disaster. None of her friends knew the identity of Belle's father, but there were those to whom she had confided that he was someone she had known in Solihull.

She closed her eyes and breathed deeply. But that shocking lie had saved her. And not only as regarded the secret of her daughter. The moment she had uttered it and seen the expression on Falco's face and known that the wall that had stood between them, which had come so close to being demolished, was now once more safely back in place, she'd felt a surge of more personal, bitter-sweet relief. For what had passed between them this afternoon deeply troubled her.

They had come so close to—what? A reconciliation? The word sent a rush of bitterness through her. A reconciliation between herself and Falco was something that would never happen. There had been too much hate, too much hurt, too much deception for such an eventuality ever to be possible. Even if she should desire it. Which she most emphatically did not.

And yet she could not deny that something had happened this afternoon. Something astonishing and cathartic and deeply unsettling. What had happened was tenderness and understanding. Briefly, the black curtain of hatred had been lifted.

This afternoon had been almost like the old days. When they'd kissed in the water, as they'd lain together on the rocks, she'd felt a closeness between them so intense and so natural that just to remember it now caused her to shudder.

And it had felt good. She could not deny that. She'd felt a peace within her, as she'd lain there, relaxing and confiding, in his arms, that she had not felt for a very long time. Not since the last time they'd lain together like that.

Was that really true? The admission slightly shocked her. It made the last three years sound sad and barren. And they had not been that. They'd been busy and fruitful.

She frowned up at the night sky. They'd been self-sufficient years. Years that had taught her how magnificently she could cope without the dubious comfort of some treacherous man.

Then she sighed. But they had, at times, been a little lonely.

That thought held her for a moment, then she pushed it aside and gazed defiantly up at the stars. Whatever had provoked her confession this afternoon it most definitely had not been some secret desire to pave the way to reconciliation! It had simply been time that the truth be spoken—at least, that part of the truth that could be spoken.

She had never taken a penny of Oscar's money. She was not the sort of person who could be bought. She owed it to herself that that finally be made clear.

Laura sighed. The night air was warm and balmy. It seemed to wrap around her like gossamer wings. She gazed out towards the sea, dark and glistening beneath the stars, and decided she'd been right to set him straight about that.

But all the other lies that divided them must remain. Because of Belle and because of what had happened this afternoon. For what had happened this afternoon must never happen again.

Laura felt a clench of remembered passion. For a moment, as she gripped the balcony railing, flames licked her senses, stirring the blood within her. She could feel the heat of Falco's lips against her lips, the power of those lean, hard, supple limbs, and the longing she had felt, intense and uncontrollable, to be consumed by that power, to surrender to it totally.

A coldness touched her, returning her to her senses. That was part of the reason why the wall must remain, in order to preserve a distance between them, in order that such madness might never occur again. For she sensed that he hated her for her supposed infidelity even more than he had hated her for supposedly taking the money.

The latter, understandably, had undermined his belief in her. The first had been a direct blow to his male ego. As long as he continued to believe she had rejected him, so quickly, so callously, for another lover—a lover to whom she had even borne a child—the barrier that divided them would remain strong and intact. And both she and Janine would be safer for that.

A frown furrowed her brow as she remembered how Janine had been waiting for them, anxious-faced, when they had arrived back at the villa. She felt a rush of guilt. Janine was so vulnerable. She'd be shattered if she knew what had been happening behind her back.

But it would never happen again. Laura firmed her lips decisively. She owed it to Janine and she owed it to herself.

It almost seemed as though Falco had come to the same decision. Over the next few days, although he was around quite a lot, he was rarely around when Laura was there.

As soon as she walked into a room, he contrived to walk out of it. When she walked out, he walked in.

Down on the beach, if Laura was lying sunbathing, Falco would be in the sea, windsurfing or swimming. Then, as soon as she put as much as her toe in the water, he would be heading back to dry land again.

He did not actively snub her. He was too subtle for that. As they passed one another in some doorway or down at the beach on the water's edge, he would always nod politely and pause to exchange a few words.

'How's the work going?' was a standby favourite.

And she would answer, 'It's going fine, thanks. I've got quite a few ideas on the boil.'

'Good. I look forward to hearing all about them. Just give me a shout whenever you're ready.'

'I shall,' she would assure him, as they went their separate ways.

Laura couldn't have asked for a more agreeable arrangement. It suited her perfectly. That was what she kept telling herself. Yet, all the same, there was something oddly undermining about his apparent anxiety to fall in with her unspoken wishes. Did he have to be *quite* so thorough about it? she wondered.

And there had been another development she could not help noting. Falco was spending a great deal more time with Janine.

Laura watched them now from beneath her sun umbrella, as the two huddled together, deep in con-

versation, on the little wooden raft, used for sunbathing and diving, which was moored a couple of
hundred metres out to sea. They'd been doing a lot
of huddling together lately, always out of earshot
of Laura, and whatever was passing between them
seemed to be doing Janine good. She had developed a new confidence in her step. Her features
fairly glowed with radiant happiness.

'We're going for a picnic lunch,' Falco had an-
nounced just yesterday when he and Janine had
emerged out on to the patio to find Laura seated
there with her sketchpad. 'I'd ask you to join us,
but I can see you're busy.'

'Oh, I am. I'm trying to get some of my ideas
down on paper. I'll fix myself a snack a little later.'

'You're sure?'

'Quite sure.' She'd smiled as she said it. Don't
worry, she'd assured him with her eyes, knowing
perfectly well the game they were playing, I
wouldn't dream of breaking in on your happy little
twosome—and I know you don't want me tagging
along!

Then she'd turned to Janine. 'Enjoy your picnic.'

Janine had grinned back at her. 'We'll see you
later.' And there was a genuine sparkle in the grey
eyes. Of that haunted, little-girl-lost look no sign
at all.

Laura had felt glad for her. The girl deserved a
break.

She smiled to herself now, a wry little smile. It
was also good to see that Falco was capable of behaving decently. Although, she found herself
amending, she had always known he was. He wasn't
all bad. Far from it. When he wanted to, he could

be the nicest, kindest man alive. When he wanted to he had in abundance what it took to make a woman happy.

The thought caused an odd sensation to go through her. A mixture of tenderness and fleeting sorrow. For the first time for a long while she found herself regretting that things had gone so disastrously wrong between them. Those early months of their relationship had been the happiest of her life.

But that was not a thought to dwell on. She pushed it from her hurriedly and replaced it with another that was much more relevant.

In the end what he had inflicted on her was pain and misery that had endured far longer than that brief taste of happiness. It was weak and foolish of her even to allow herself to recall those all-too-brief happy months.

But the memory of them lingered as her gaze flickered out to sea again, to the two huddled figures on the raft. And again she felt it, that cold touch of loneliness, that sense of something lacking in her life, a lack she had never before admitted to herself.

And for the first time ever she found herself asking why she had allowed no other man to fill the void. Plenty, after all, had offered themselves.

Because of Belle and because I like things as they are, she answered herself instantly, automatically, yet wondering as a cold chill settled round her heart why that declaration suddenly no longer rang true.

It was the following morning that Falco approached her. As Laura was finishing breakfast alone on the terrace, he appeared from the drawing-room and came to stand before her.

'I was wondering if you were ready to discuss your ideas? Janine's gone into the village to do a bit of shopping. So we're on our own. I thought it would be a good opportunity.'

'Of course. I'll get my sketches.'

'Finish your breakfast first.' As she half rose to her feet, he waved her back into her seat. 'I might even join you for a coffee,' he added, stepping forward and seating himself in one of the chairs opposite her.

'Of course.' Laura pushed the coffee-pot towards him. 'I think there's enough there for a couple of cups.'

Wasn't it a little odd, she found herself wondering, as she glanced down at her croissant, suddenly aware that her appetite had abruptly deserted her, that he should prefer to discuss her ideas in Janine's absence? Most men, in her experience, preferred to include their girlfriends in the process of decorating their houses.

But then Falco wasn't most men, she quickly reminded herself. And this was simply another manifestation of his ambivalence when it came to close relationships.

One foot in and one foot out. That was as close to commitment as he ever seemed to get—though he was adroit at giving quite a different impression. Like herself three years ago, Janine was probably under the misapprehension—especially after his attentiveness over the past few days—that she was a fixed and vital element in his life.

Laura watched him as he poured his coffee and took a mouthful, resenting the uneasiness his proximity stirred in her. This was the first time they had been alone together since that afternoon out on the rock. All at once, deep inside, she was in a turmoil of emotion.

Falco, however, betrayed no emotion as he turned to her. 'I hope you're enjoying your stay on Alba? I hope you're managing to relax a bit as well as work?'

'Oh, yes.' His detachment was oddly undermining. 'It's a very beautiful island. You're very lucky.'

'I suppose.' He regarded her for a moment. 'I suppose all of us are lucky in our different ways.' He leaned back in his chair as she wondered what he'd meant by that and, without altering his tone one tiny fraction, proceeded to hit her with a thuderbolt.

'Why didn't you tell me you had a little girl?'

'Of what possible interest could it be to you?' In spite of her shock, she shot the answer back at him. Her eyes looked steadily back into his. 'The details of my personal life are really none of your business.'

'Granted.' He took another mouthful of his coffee. 'But most mothers, in my experience, are only too happy for any opportunity to talk about their offspring.'

Laura smiled to herself. She definitely fell into that category! There were few things she enjoyed more than talking about Belle.

But she continued to regard Falco with stiff hostility. 'Perhaps I'm selective about who I discuss my daughter with.'

Something touched his eyes, like a fleeting cloud against the sun. Then it was gone as he said, 'You would have discussed her with my friends—my American friends who were here the other day. In fact, you very nearly did.'

So, he *had* picked up her slip and it had stayed in his memory. She ought to have known that he was simply biding his time.

Laura said, glancing away, feeling momentarily awkward, 'I was talking to another mother who was missing her child. All I said was that I understood how she felt.'

'Yes, you did. Then you instantly withdrew the remark. You pretended that what you'd meant was that you could "imagine" how she felt.' His dark eyes pierced her. 'Wasn't that an odd thing to do?'

'On the surface it may seem so.' Laura was floundering. 'But the reason I did that...' She stopped floundering and spoke boldly. Through boldness, she sensed, lay her only escape. 'The reason I did that was to cover my tracks. I was hoping you might not have noticed my slip. As I suggested earlier, the subject of my daughter is not one I have any desire to discuss with you.'

In silence the dark eyes regarded her for a moment. Then in a quiet tone he put to her, 'Why is that? Were you afraid I might disapprove of your being a single mother?'

Such arrogance! 'Why should I care if you disapprove or not? As I keep telling you, my private life is none of your business.'

But he continued as though she had not spoken. 'For I can assure you I don't disapprove in the slightest. In fact, I have a great deal of admiration for any girl who has the guts to bring up a child on her own.'

He paused as she looked back at him in surprise at this compliment. Then he added in an altogether grittier tone, 'The only thing I disapprove of is your choice of father.'

'Yes, that was unfortunate. I'm afraid it was an accident.'

'That much I'd assumed.' He sat back in his seat and looked at her. 'So, how old is your daughter, this secret Belle of yours?'

Laura thought quickly. 'Just two,' she answered. In fact, Belle was now nearly two and a half. But Falco was notoriously good at sums.

Falco nodded. 'You told me you'd lost contact with the father. In a way, I think that's a little bit unfortunate. The role of father is a role that's sometimes underrated, but personally I think it's a most important one. I know I could never walk away from any child of mine.'

Laura's heart was suddenly huge in her chest. She could feel it pressing against her ribs. She looked into his face through a blur of emotion. She had known that. She had feared that. That was why she kept her secret. And yet, illogically, she felt a flood of warmth towards him. She had told herself he might try to take Belle out of spite. But her real fear had been, though she had never acknowledged it, that he might try to take her out of love.

There was an endless silence as they sat and looked at one another. Time lay suspended all around them. Then, very quietly, Falco said, 'Why did you tell me you'd taken that money? That day in London when I came to find you, why didn't you simply say it wasn't true?'

Laura took a deep breath. 'I was angry,' she answered him. 'Angry and hurt that you could believe such a thing of me. The way you accused me, the way you started yelling at me...'

'That was because of that so-called evidence my father had shown me. I explained all of that to you just the other day.'

'But I didn't know it then. I didn't know about the faked evidence. All I knew was that you were yelling and shouting and accusing me of being a money-grabbing tramp.'

Falco sighed. 'Yes, I confess I did express myself rather strongly.' Then he shook his head. 'But you could have denied it. You could have put me straight right there and then.'

'No, I couldn't. I had my father to think of.'

'You could have told me you hadn't taken the money without danger of jeopardising your father.'

'I couldn't. You would have started asking questions. You would have wondered why your own father had bothered to lie to you. Of course there was a danger of it rebounding on my father.'

Falco narrowed his black eyes at her. 'Sure, I would have asked questions ... but why would they necessarily have led back to your father? I didn't know about my father's threat to fire him. You hadn't told me and there was no one else who could.'

He paused. 'And I think you know as well as I do that my father would have had no problem whatsoever inventing some excuse for his lie about the money. All that mattered to him, from what you've told me, was that you get out of my life. And you'd already done that.'

He shook his head. 'No, it just doesn't make sense. It just doesn't make sense that you didn't deny you'd taken the money.'

It would have made sense if he knew the truth. The thought beat like a drum inside her head. If he knew what it felt like to love someone so desperately that the only thing that mattered in the world was that person. If he knew what it felt like to believe that that person loved and trusted you as deeply as you loved and trusted them. And then to have that person hurl such hurts and accusations, to behave like a stranger, and, worse, a hated enemy. If he had known all that, he would have understood the total, unbearable sense of desolation that had rendered her incapable of defending herself, that had caused her to hate him and strike out to wound him with that lie that had felt like a knife plunging into her own heart.

Laura could scarcely breathe. Her heart was racing. Though, as he spoke now, Falco's words almost caused it to stop.

He said, 'The truth is I didn't really believe it...about you taking the money...until you actually told me you did. I know I accused you...I remember what I said... But all the time I was hoping—in fact, I was *certain*—that you would tell me it was all a load of nonsense.'

Laura turned away, fearfully rejecting what he was saying. 'It didn't sound that way,' she responded a little croakily.

'Are you surprised? Have you ever stopped to think how *I* was feeling?' The emotion in his voice caused her to snap back to look at him. 'I'd just got back from a routine business trip to find a letter from you saying the romance was over. Just like that, you'd stepped out of my life, leaving no address, no nothing. Did you ever stop to wonder what that did to me?'

The truth was she hadn't. Or, if she had, she'd just assumed that he'd cope with it in the same way he coped with everything. With poise and self-assurance. That he'd simply come and look for her. It had never crossed her mind that he might be devastated.

He was continuing, 'When your parents refused to tell me where you were, the first thing I did was approach my father.' A cold smile touched his eyes as he elaborated briefly, 'I knew from experience he tends to be at the back of most things. And that, of course, was when he told me about the money he'd given you and showed me his copy of the banker's draft as proof.'

His eyes became hard. 'If I'd believed him,' he continued, 'I wouldn't have spent the next six weeks scouring the country, trying to track you down.' His tone was self-mocking. 'I looked absolutely everywhere, almost literally from Land's End to John-o'-Groats. In the end I decided to concentrate on London. That's where most runaways end up. And in the end I found you—ironically, with the help of my father. He recommended I use a detective agency. And I did. And they came up with the goods.'

Laura's heart was suddenly beating so hard that she felt it might suddenly burst out of her chest.

I'm sorry. More than anything, she wanted to say it. The picture he'd just painted made her heart sore. It had never crossed her mind the trouble he must have gone to and the agony he must have suffered in his efforts to track her down.

She'd been naïve. She'd believed him to be superhuman. She'd believed him to be invulnerable. And she could see that she had hurt him.

Laura opened her mouth to put those feelings into words, but before she could he was speaking again.

'I was convinced it was a lie, about the money. I was convinced there had to be another reason ...' He paused on a sigh. 'And, of course, I was right.'

A frown touched her brow. For a moment, quite genuinely, Laura failed totally to grasp his meaning.

In a crisp tone, he explained. 'You simply wanted your freedom. Freedom to experiment sexually, among other things. And you hadn't wasted any time. By the time I found you, you'd already fixed yourself up with another boyfriend.'

A vision swam before her of the man in question and of the situation in which Falco had seen them together. The dealer had been ushering her into his Jaguar, a little too solicitously, she remembered, before whisking her off to his Chelsea showroom. It had been an unfortunate occurrence, but scant evidence, surely, for the damning conclusions that Falco had come to?

Which took them more or less straight back to square one. She might have misjudged him with her assumption that he'd had no good reason to believe she'd taken the money, but she had not misjudged him with regard to the antiques dealer. On what was virtually no proof at all, he had believed the worst and accused her accordingly.

He was accusing her now, his tone tight with distaste. 'Couldn't you at least have found yourself a more palatable lover?'

'I found him perfectly palatable.' Her sense of guilt had eased a little. She spoke the rebuttal as though she really meant it.

Falco regarded her narrowly. 'I suppose that's understandable. As you were so keen to inform me, he had certain talents in the bedroom. His performance must really have been quite something to persuade you to overlook his other less desirable characteristics.'

'Yes, it must have been.' Her facial muscles felt tight. The way she was forced to keep confirming this lie made her feel almost physically sick. For Falco was right—and what sharp eyes he had to have judged the dealer so accurately on one brief glimpse!—the man had been sleazy, unpalatable and offensive, the last man in the world she was ever likely to have gone to bed with.

Falco said, 'Ah, well, it must have been nice for you to have someone who was a good lover for a change.'

He had thrown the remark at her as though he didn't care. And perhaps he didn't. It was impossible to tell. But all the same it shamed her. She should never have said that. She could never know a better lover than Falco.

'Falco, I——'

But, before she could speak, with a sudden brusque movement he was rising to his feet, as though he were shrugging her off. 'I suggest you go and get your sketches,' he was saying. 'I'll see you in the drawing-room. We can discuss them there.'

'Falco...' Overcome with remorse, she rose to face him. There had been wrongs on both sides, but in so many ways she had wounded him far more deeply than she had ever intended.

He was glancing at his watch, deliberately ignoring her. 'I can give you an hour, then I have things I have to do.'

'Falco...' He was about to step away from the table. She had to stop him. She reached out her hand. 'Falco, I'm sorry.' Her hand closed around his arm. 'Falco, I'm sorry,' she said again.

'Sorry for what?' The dark eyes were shuttered. His tone was tight. 'Sorry for what?'

'Sorry for what I put you through. I handled things badly...'

'You mean you ought to have made a cleaner, tidier break?'

'No, I didn't mean that.' Her heart was pounding and, though she was quite unaware of it, her grip on his arm had tightened.

'Then what did you mean?'

She was weeping inside. If only she could tell him the whole, uncensored story. 'I'm sorry I had to hurt you. I never meant to hurt you. You were always so good to me. I should have been kinder.'

'Kinder? There's no kind way of breaking off a romance. And that was what you wanted. You were probably right to be ruthless.'

Laura shook her head. 'It hurt me too, you know. It wasn't easy for me. It really wasn't easy.'

'Why, if it was what you wanted?' He had turned to face her. 'If it was what you wanted, it ought to have been easy.'

'It ought...' Laura could scarcely bear to look at him. She longed to say, But it wasn't what I wanted. And she had a strong sense that he was willing her to say it.

But she couldn't say it. It would open the floodgates. She bit her lip and looked back at him in silence, the agony in her soul pouring from her eyes.

Falco frowned then. And suddenly the arm she held so tightly had moved to circle round her waist.

He shook his head. 'I can't shake off the feeling that none of this makes any sense.' Then he sighed. 'Does any of it make any sense to you?'

Laura shook her head, scarcely daring to look at him. 'Sometimes I think the whole world makes no sense.'

'Except now. This minute.' He cupped her chin with his hand, forcing her to look at him, and smiled a strange smile. 'This moment, just possibly, makes a little sense.'

'Just possibly.' She found herself smiling back at him. A warm sensation had gathered round her heart.

For a moment they just stood there, eyes locked together. Then with breathtaking gentleness he gathered her against him and bent to kiss her softly on the lips.

Laura could feel his heartbeat as they clung together, and she could sense his need, more spiritual than physical, that seemed identically to match her own. She wanted that kiss to last forever. Its magical gentleness seemed to heal her soul.

And suddenly in her heart she felt a dart of longing to tear down the wall of falsehoods and misunderstandings that, in spite of this moment, still stood between them.

But then, right on cue, in response to some sixth sense, she found herself glancing over his shoulder.

And her heart stopped dead as she found herself looking into Janine's wide, startled eyes.

CHAPTER NINE

JANINE seemed to freeze in the doorway for a split second, as though unable to believe what she was seeing. Then she was turning on her heel with a hoarse little cry and rushing, as though pursued, back into the house.

Laura watched the girl's flight with a sense of stricken horror. Again, despite her promises, she'd done Janine wrong.

Laura tore herself free from Falco's embrace. 'I'm going after her, to apologise!' she proclaimed.

But Falco had grabbed hold of her, his grip tight around her arm. 'Let her go. It doesn't matter. Stop making a fuss about nothing.'

Nothing, he called it! Laura felt horror turn to anger. His girlfriend had just caught him embracing another woman and he had the nerve to call it nothing!

With a surge of furious strength she tore her arm free. 'You're a cold-hearted bastard!' Her blue eyes sparked furiously. 'But I don't care what you say, I'm going after her. She deserves an explanation and an apology!'

Then she was swinging away from him and racing after Janine. 'Wait!' she was calling. 'Wait, Janine!'

But she was too late. She heard the front door slam. Then, a moment later, as she snatched it open and went rushing out into the forecourt, she saw

Janine, already behind the wheel of her car, head off with a squeal of tyres down the driveway.

'Janine! Come back!' Though she knew it was hopeless, waving her arms frantically, Laura rushed after her. 'Come back! Come back! Let me explain!'

'You're wasting your time.' Falco was standing in the doorway. Laura spun round in her tracks at the sound of his voice and saw with a sense of shock that he was smiling. 'My guess is that she's heading for the jetty.' He glanced at his watch with an air of casual indifference. 'There's a ferry due to sail out in a couple of minutes.'

'Can I borrow your car?' Laura snapped the question at him. 'I'd like to try and stop her. In case she does something stupid.'

'She won't do anything stupid.' Falco continued to smile that amused, uncaring, heartless smile. 'But if you want, you're welcome to borrow the car. You'll find the keys in the ignition.'

'Thank you.' Laura's tone was as brittle as crystal. Then without another glance at him—the sight of him enraged her—she was hurrying across the forecourt to where the car was parked, jumping behind the wheel and switching on the engine. She stepped hard on the accelerator and headed off towards the road.

It was fortunate that she met no other traffic on the way, for the island's roads were narrow, not designed for speed, and Laura drove like a demon the five kilometres to the little jetty. It was the only way she had any hope of catching up with Janine and stopping her before the ferry sailed.

For she sensed Falco had been right and that was where Janine was headed. She'd had that look of a woman fleeing.

And, indeed, there she was, already aboard the ferry, as in a cloud of dust Laura drew up alongside.

She wound down the window. 'Wait for me!' she called. But she was already too late. The ferryman had drawn up the gangplank and the little vessel was moving rapidly away from the shore.

'I'll be back in about an hour!' the ferryman called to her. 'I can take you over then!'

An hour! Laura cursed and banged her fist on the steering-wheel. Who knew where, and in what state, Janine would be by then?

In helpless frustration she sat in the car and watched as the ferry moved further and further away. What have I done to that poor girl? she thought forlornly. For she, as much as Falco, was to blame.

The ferry was now little more than a speck on the horizon. What should I do now? Laura wondered as she watched it. What can I do to set this mess right?

She turned the car around and headed back to the villa. If only I could leave, she found herself wishing again, tears springing to her eyes, tears of despair. These moments of intimacy between herself and Falco were becoming more frequent the longer she stayed. He did nothing to prevent them, and she found herself unable to. It was like something in her blood, something she could not fight against. She still responded to Falco just as she had in the old days.

That thought pierced her like hot needles as she headed back to the villa. Of course, she did not love him. It was not a question of love. But something, something powerful, still existed between them. Something that in some rash moment might lead her to confess her secret. And something that, in addition, had already wounded Janine.

An idea was starting to take shape in her head. Perhaps the solution was indeed for her to leave. After all, if she did, what was the worst thing that could happen? That Falco would keep his threat to go to London and start stirring things up among her colleagues. But if she got there first and rang round all her intimates, swearing them to silence on the subject of Belle, perhaps she need have nothing to fear.

There was always a risk, of course. There were always people who liked to talk, and you could never be sure whom you could trust. That was what had held her back from making this decision in the first place.

But at this moment she wasn't sure she could even trust herself. The risks either way—whether she left or stayed—on balance, were beginning to feel about even. And it would be such a tremendous relief to go.

Laura's mind was made up as she reached the villa. She would write Janine a note and leave immediately. If she was quick, she might manage to catch the next ferry.

She drew to a halt and pulled on the handbrake. Goodbye, Alba. Goodbye, Falco. It was the right decision and she would allow nothing to stop her.

*   *   *

'Might I enquire what you think you're up to?' Suddenly, a pair of dark eyes were watching her from the doorway. 'It looks suspiciously to me as though you're packing.'

'That's exactly what I'm doing.' Laura did not turn round, but continued to concentrate on the pile of skirts and blouses that she was dumping unceremoniously into the suitcase on her bed.

'And why are you packing?'

'Because I'm leaving.'

'Leaving? Why? You can't leave yet. Your two weeks aren't nearly up yet.'

'I'm leaving anyway.' Still, she did not look at him. She grabbed a pile of T-shirts and dropped them in the case. 'I'm leaving on the very next ferry.'

There was a pause. Laura sensed that he had stepped into the room. She could feel his closeness, dark and oppressive. He said, 'I repeat, you can't leave yet. We have an agreement. You're to stay two weeks.'

'I'm breaking the agreement.' Laura did turn round then. 'I'm breaking the agreement and I'm leaving right now.' Her blue eyes narrowed. 'Don't try to stop me.'

'Does that mean that you're turning down the commission?' Falco was standing midway between the door and the bed, his hands in the pockets of his cream linen trousers. 'Is that what you're doing? Reneging on our contract?'

A sudden thought occurred to her. 'Not necessarily,' Laura told him. 'I'm prepared to honour our contract, but only on one condition——'

'What condition?'

'On condition that I have the house to myself. That is...that you promise not to be here while I'm working.'

Falco laughed then, as she had more or less expected he would. 'And why would I agree to such a preposterous condition? In case you had forgotten, this does happen to be my house.'

'I'm aware of that.' Laura slammed down the lid of her suitcase. 'But that's my condition and I'm afraid I insist on it absolutely.'

'I see.' As he spoke, he took his hands from his pockets and folded his arms across his chest. 'And is there any particular reason for the sudden imposition of this quite unacceptable condition?'

'I think you know what my reasons are. And, if you don't, you ought to.' With a movement that could only be described as vicious she snatched the zip of her suitcase closed. 'I don't really think there's any need to discuss them.'

'Oh, you don't?'

'No, I don't.' Laura grabbed the suitcase by its handle and swung it from the bed down on to the floor.

'Just like that, you plan to break our agreement...you plan to walk out without even giving me notice...and you don't think there's any need for discussion...?'

Laura felt her lips purse. He was blocking her exit.

Falco smiled. 'Do you seriously think I'm going to allow this to happen?'

It was a rhetorical question. The answer was in his eyes. Laura dropped her suitcase to the floor and glared at him. 'I'm leaving because of Janine,' she snapped impatiently. It was part of the truth and all he needed to know. 'I'm leaving because of your behaviour... and because of mine,' she added swiftly. 'I don't like the way things are going between us. I don't want to be responsible for Janine getting hurt. If you had any decency, you'd see that it's best. If you had any conscience, you wouldn't try to stop me.'

She took a deep breath and retrieved her suitcase. 'There,' she concluded, 'you've had your discussion. Now kindly step aside and let me past.'

'Not yet.' Falco's arms remained firmly folded across his chest. 'I'm afraid that wasn't what I'd call a discussion. A discussion is when two people each have a say. You still haven't heard what I think about all this.'

'Do I really need to?' Laura's blue eyes scowled at him. 'We both know that what I've just said is right.'

'About Janine, you mean? About our duty to her?' Falco raised black eyebrows. 'Is that what you're talking about?'

Laura's lips pursed tighter. 'You know it's what I'm talking about!'

'In that case...' He smiled and unfolded his arms.

Laura felt her heart lift. Was he about to move aside? Tentatively, hopefully, she took a step forward.

And that was precisely the moment he chose to reach out and snatch the suitcase from her hand. 'In that case,' he told her, tossing the suitcase into a corner, 'our discussion, I'm sorry to tell you, hasn't even started.'

Before she could react, he had caught hold of her arm and was smiling with amusement into her eyes. 'So, where would you prefer we have our discussion? Here or downstairs in the drawing-room?'

'What discussion? There's nothing to discuss!' Laura made a violent, but futile effort to free herself. 'Let go of my arm! What the devil do you think you're doing?'

'Here or downstairs in the drawing-room?' He repeated his question without releasing his grip one centimetre. Then, as she continued to struggle in speechless anger, he provided his own answer.

'I think the drawing-room might be preferable. You can have a drink while we talk. I have a feeling you're going to need one.'

And what was that supposed to mean? Laura continued to struggle futilely. 'Let me go! We have absolutely nothing to discuss! All you're going to do is make me miss my ferry!'

'Then you can catch a later one.' He had no intention of releasing her. Already, he was dragging her out on to the landing. 'Now, do I have to carry you downstairs, or will you walk?'

'I'll walk, thank you!' Laura had given up struggling. It was a waste of effort and, besides, her arm was hurting. She glared at him, daring him to inflict on her the indignity of being thrown over his shoulder and carried down bodily to the drawing-room. 'You can cut the he-man act,' she told him crisply.

That simply amused him. 'It's entirely up to you. If you want to behave like a wayward child, that's precisely how I'll treat you.'

Laura refrained from responding, but made her way down the stairs, then turned and headed for the drawing-room. Her plan now was to listen to whatever he had to say to her, then leave, as she had intended, on the first ferry available.

She seated herself in one of the damask-covered armchairs and watched from beneath her lashes as Falco crossed to the bar. Intense irritation was all she was feeling. Not even the tiniest spark of curiosity.

Falco asked her, 'What do you fancy? Campari and soda?'

Laura eyed him with hostility. 'A glass of mineral water would be sufficient.'

'If that's what you want...but I would advise something a little stronger.' He smiled as he said it. He was enjoying this little game of his.

Laura looked right back at him. 'In that case, *you* have something stronger. I'm sure *I'll* find a glass of mineral water perfectly sufficient.'

'If you say so.' He continued to smile infuriatingly as he tossed ice-cubes into two glasses then, with a flourish, poured mineral water into one of them and a small measure of whisky into the other.

He crossed the room and handed Laura her glass. 'Cheers!' he said. 'Or, as they say in these parts, *salute*!'

Laura very pointedly did not return the toast. She took a sip of her mineral water, regarding him with displeasure as he seated himself calmly in the armchair opposite her. She said, 'So, what was it that was so vital that you had to keep me here to hear it?'

Falco watched her for a moment. He was not about to be hurried. He took a mouthful of his whisky, seemed to savour it, then swallowed. Then he leaned back more comfortably against the chair cushions. 'Were you planning,' he put to her, 'just to go off without a word to me? That strikes me as a little unprofessional, not to say lamentably ill-mannered.'

With difficulty, Laura suppressed a sigh of impatience. 'Is this what you brought me down here to discuss? If it is, I can give you my answer in five seconds. Yes, I was planning to leave without telling you. Forgive my bad manners, but I really thought it would be best.'

'Best for whom?'

'Best for all of us. And don't ask me why. I've already explained my reasons.'

'And what about the job you came here to do? What was I supposed to think when I discovered you'd gone? Was I supposed to hang around and see if you'd bother to come back or was I supposed to go out and find myself another decorator?'

'I planned to phone you from the mainland, or write you a letter, and explain to you exactly what I explained to you upstairs—that I was prepared to do the job, but only on condition——'

'That I absent myself from my own house,' he finished for her. He threw her an amused look. 'And all of this because your conscience was suddenly bothering you regarding Janine?'

Laura threw him a hard look. 'Go on, laugh!' she taunted. 'I didn't expect for one moment that you would understand such feelings.'

Falco obliged her by laughing. 'This is all very flattering.' He let his eyes travel unhurriedly over her face, then sweep lower to subject the rest of her to his scrutiny. 'What you're more or less saying is that if you were to stay on here in my company you would find yourself unable to keep your hands off me.'

Laura flushed a deep scarlet. 'That is not what I'm saying! I assure you I'm saying nothing of the kind!'

Falco feigned incomprehension. 'It seemed so to me. That seemed to me precisely what you were saying.'

'Well, it wasn't!'

'Then why the need to flee? The only reason you were fleeing was because of these uncontrollable urges.'

Laura's fingers had tightened around her glass, and suddenly she was wishing that, after all, it did contain something a little stronger than water. Vitriol. To throw in his face!

In measured tones she told him, breathing slowly, 'I'm not the one with uncontrollable impulses. You're the one who seems to suffer from that problem. Every time we're alone together you keep on making passes at me.'

'Which you, of course, rebuff.'

'I've tried to. Sometimes.'

Laura dropped her eyes to her lap as she said it. The irony in his tone, after all, was justified. She hadn't exactly fought him off with tooth and claw. She looked across at him now, a sudden sadness sweeping through her, momentarily replacing the anger and humiliation. Once, such a conversation would have been unthinkable between them. Once, they had each rejoiced in the physical passion of the other. And that still somehow seemed much more natural than this.

Falco swirled the ice-cubes round in his glass, apparently unafflicted by such regrets. On the contrary, he appeared to be enjoying himself hugely.

He crossed one leg at the ankle over the knee of the other and put to her, 'So, in order to avoid doing wrong to Janine, you decided the only solution was to cut and run?'

Laura shrugged. 'I'm not sure what you mean by doing wrong.' She flushed as she said it. Did he delude himself, she wondered, that she might have allowed him to make love to her if she had stayed? She added quickly, 'The only wrongs I was afraid of doing were the kind we had already committed.'

Falco nodded, watching her, smiling with amusement. 'Your sense of moral responsibility towards others really does you credit,' he told her.

'Which is more,' Laura informed him cuttingly, 'than can be said of yours.' His whole attitude to this affair was downright disgraceful.

He simply continued to smile that uncaring, callous smile of his. 'I must tell Janine all about this when she comes back.'

Laura was stunned for a moment. His shamelessness was shocking. Yet she felt oddly relieved that the conversation had changed direction.

'And how do you know she'll come back?' Her tone was full of censure. 'Perhaps you've upset her so much that she'll stay away for good. Or worse. Pray God I'm wrong, but what if she does herself some harm?'

Falco simply shook his head. 'Don't worry about that.' There was not even a glimmer of concern in his tone. 'I'm sure the last thing on her mind is doing herself harm.'

'And how can you be so sure?'

'Because I know why she's gone.' His smile grew broader. 'And I know who she's with.'

He was talking in riddles now. Laura laid down her glass and leaned towards him, frowning, as she asked, 'What are you talking about? Who is she with?'

'Her boyfriend.'

'Her boyfriend? I thought *you* were her boyfriend?'

'I know that's what you thought, but that has never been the case. Janine and I have never had that sort of relationship.'

'I don't believe you!' Laura fell back in her seat, her eyes fixed on his face, searching for the truth. 'She told me you did! She told me she adores you! I saw you together. Don't try to deny it!'

'But I do deny it. I deny it absolutely.' Suddenly Falco was no longer smiling. He laid down his glass and breathed in deeply. 'If Janine told you she adores me, I'm deeply flattered. But I tend to think she was exaggerating just a little. She feels grateful to me...' He smiled and added, 'And tends to be quite uninhibited about showing it.' Then, more soberly, he continued, 'And I, for my part, feel great tenderness towards her.'

Laura was totally baffled. She leaned towards him once again, knowing, without understanding, that he was speaking the truth. 'What are you talking about?' she demanded softly. 'What reason has Janine to feel grateful to you?'

He did not answer immediately. He picked up his whisky glass, gazed into its contents for a moment, then drank. Laura could sense he was debating how much he should tell her. Then he glanced up into her eyes and in a steely tone told her, 'Janine was my father's discarded mistress.'

Laura looked back at him, a sense of shock driving through her. In silence she listened as he continued,

'I found out about her through a friend of mine a couple of months ago. She was in a terrible state. Suicidal. My father had treated her pretty badly.' He took a deep breath. 'So, I brought her here and told her she could stay until she had recovered.

'It was an uphill job, trying to restore her confidence. She'd lost faith in herself totally. Her self-esteem was down to zero. But little by little, she began to make progress. Little by little, she came out of her depression.' A light smile touched his eyes. 'I think she's OK now.'

Suddenly, all the pieces were falling into place. The almost parental affection Falco showed towards Janine. Janine's claim that he had turned her whole life around. Laura felt her heart swell with emotion inside her. Tears pricked her eyes. He had done a wonderful thing.

She swallowed. 'So, who's this boyfriend you mentioned? The one you said she's gone to see.'

Falco drained his whisky and laid down the empty glass. He smiled. 'An old flame. Someone she almost married before she got involved with my father. He came back on the scene just a short while ago. First came a letter, then a phone call...' He paused. 'You were here the night of the phone call. That was when he told her he was coming to Italy to see her.'

Laura bit her lip in shame. She remembered that phone call and what had happened after Janine had gone to take it. That was when she'd thrown the wine in Falco's face.

She said now, 'What a fool I've been. I jumped to all the wrong conclusions. I suppose what happened this afternoon was that she received some message that the boyfriend was on his way and came to tell you she was going off to meet him...'

'Then she found us—shall we say?—sharing a somewhat private moment, decided not to interrupt us and rushed off to catch the ferry...' Falco nodded. 'Yes, that was my interpretation.'

'Oh, lord, you must think me a perfect idiot!' Laura covered her face with her hands and shook her head. Then, through her fingers, she looked across at Falco. 'But you knew I believed that you and Janine were involved and you allowed me to go on believing it. Why didn't you tell me I was wrong right from the beginning?'

'Do you think I ought to have?'

'Most definitely I think so! You let me believe you were two-timing Janine!'

Falco had leaned forward in his seat, both feet on the floor now, his hands clasped together and dropped down between his knees. The dark eyes held hers, seeming to pour through her. 'Surely you knew that wasn't my style. I'm guilty of many sins, but I've never been a philanderer. Was I ever unfaithful to you?'

'No.' Laura shook her head. 'No, you weren't.'

The way he was looking at her was making her skin burn. Her heart seemed to have risen and lodged in her throat. How wonderful he is, she kept thinking to herself. And how I have misjudged him, this wonderful, caring man. This wonderful, caring man who is the father of my child.

She wanted to reach out to him and feel his arms wrap around her, to touch his face, caress his hair and press her lips adoringly against the tiny dark mole in the corner of his left eye.

Restraining herself, she said, 'I'm sorry for the way I've acted. I ought to have known you weren't capable of behaving so badly.'

Falco nodded. 'Yes, you ought. You of all people.'

His eyes seemed to swallow her, those wondrous dark eyes of his. She could feel her soul melting as he leaned closer towards her. Then she froze as he said, his tone harsh and accusing, '*You're* the one with the taste for infidelity. Perhaps that was what caused you to make all the wrong assumptions. You made the mistake of judging me by your own low standards.'

It was as though he had thrown cold water in her face. Laura felt herself recoil. Her heart seemed to freeze over. Suddenly, uncontrollably, she was shaking all over. In an instant he had become a stranger again.

He continued to look at her. 'What do you think? Could I be right?'

Laura could not answer. Her tongue had been torn out. And, as she had expected, he interpreted her silence as agreement.

Falco rose to his feet. 'Our discussion is now over. Feel free to leave whenever you wish.'

Then, leaving her wounded and bleeding in her chair, her soul broken and weeping with despair, he turned away swiftly and strode from the room.

Laura caught the first ferry the following morning. While Janine and her boyfriend and Falco were still asleep, she climbed into a taxi and headed for the jetty, back to the mainland, never to return.

CHAPTER TEN

LAURA lay staring at the ceiling of her hotel bedroom, wishing she could sleep, knowing she could not. There were too many questions clamouring for answers in her head.

First and foremost, why was she still here? Why hadn't she grabbed the first flight back to London? Why, instead, had she checked into this *pensione* in Naples? After all, when she had fled from Alba this morning, it had been her intention to fly straight home.

Yet here she still was, though it made no sense at all. Her business in Italy was concluded. She had not one single reason to remain.

Laura squeezed her eyes closed. But something was telling her it would be wrong for her to leave this way.

She felt badly, of course, about her abandoned commission. The way it had all ended was highly unprofessional. But what choice had she had? Falco had left her no option when he had refused categorically to accept her condition that he stay away while she was working on the villa. She simply could not accept any other arrangement. To have him around her would be wrong and dangerous.

Well, perhaps not wrong, she corrected herself, frowning, now that she knew he was not involved with Janine. But that would simply make it even more dangerous than before.

With Janine no longer a factor to consider, how would she resist the power that drew them together—and that kept pushing her to the edge of confession? She would be unable to resist it. That was the answer.

That realisation bothered Laura deeply. For she knew that it meant that the attraction she felt was something far deeper than mere animal magnetism. It was something vast and warm and full of wonder. There was something magical about Falco, or about the effect he had on her. He could light up her heart as no other man could.

She allowed herself to dwell on that thought for a moment. Yesterday, she had to confess, when he had told her the story of Janine and his father and of how he, Falco, had helped her, Laura had looked into his face and felt an admiration so deep that for a moment she had almost believed she still loved him.

No, not *almost*. She *had* believed it, she corrected herself. And in that moment her heart had filled to overflowing with a happiness and a sense of wholeness she had not known for years.

Of course, he had crushed the feeling instantly with that brutal attack on her, with that familiar accusation that never failed to cut her like a knife. *You're the one with the taste for infidelity*! The look of hate in his eyes had shrivelled her soul.

Laura had told herself then that she had been mistaken. She did not love him. How could she love a man who persisted in believing her guilty of a sin he had never had cause to believe her guilty of in the first place?

She breathed in and sighed and stared once more at the ceiling. How could she love a man who was so like his hateful father that he had remained faithfully at his side for all those years, while knowing full well what type of man he was?

But he was *not* like Oscar. Her heart rejected the comparison. He was not a philanderer. He was not cold-hearted. Look at all he'd done for poor Janine! He was all she had believed yesterday. A caring, compassionate man.

With a sigh of impatience—none of it made sense, and at this rate she was never going to sleep!—Laura sat up and switched on the bedside lamp. Then she slid from the bed and crossed to the window, threw the shutters open and gazed out into the night.

A sky full of stars twinkled over the Bay of Naples. The salt tang of the sea and the sweetness of acacia blossom mingled in the clean night air. Laura breathed in deeply, her heart a tangle of emotions. There was only one solution. Tomorrow she must leave. First thing, she told herself. On the first flight available.

Yet, as she stood there, gazing out into the starry darkness, she could not quite silence the voice that kept telling her it would be wrong for her to leave this way.

It came to her quite suddenly, just before dawn.

Laura had drifted off to sleep what seemed like just a moment earlier, then suddenly she was awake again, her brain clear and functioning. Suddenly she knew why it would be wrong for her to leave now. And, though it scared her, she knew, too, what she must do.

She sat up, staring into the darkness, her fists clenched at her sides, her heart beating within her.

It was a risk, but it was a risk it was her duty to take.

He was sitting on the rock, facing out to sea, dressed in white trousers and a plain blue T-shirt, hunched a little, his strong arms wrapped around his knees.

Laura hesitated for a moment as a sudden panic gripped her. He hadn't seen her arrive and it would be so easy just to get back on her bike and head back to the villa.

But that would be weak and cowardly—and wrong. She laid down her bike and stepped towards him, a slender, nervous figure in a pink cotton sundress. 'Falco!' she called. 'Do you mind if I join you?'

He turned then, abruptly, swivelling round to face her, and for a moment regarded her in total silence. Then he turned to face the sea again. 'What's the matter?' he enquired. 'Why are you back? Is there something you've forgotten?'

Laura could feel her heart beating. He wasn't going to make this easy. But she had not expected that he would, so it made no difference.

She scrambled across the rock until she was just a few feet away from him. 'No, I haven't forgotten anything. I've come because I want to speak to you.'

He had resumed his earlier position, arms circling his knees, his gaze fixed steadfastly on the horizon. 'How did you find me?' he demanded. 'Who told you I was here?'

'Anna told me you were out. She said you'd taken the car.' Feeling awkward, Laura seated herself on the rock beside him and carefully tucked her legs beneath her. 'I guessed you'd be here.' She laughed self-consciously. 'A lucky guess.'

'That remains to be seen.' Falco kept his eyes averted. Then he enquired, 'Was there something in particular you wished to speak about?'

'As a matter of fact, yes.' Laura's gaze had never flickered. It remained fixed on the dark, implacable profile, so resolutely turned against her. But at least, she was thinking, he seemed prepared to listen. She had been a little afraid he might refuse to do even that.

'So, what is it? Is it something to do with the villa?' He slid her a look then, dark and closely shuttered. 'If it is, that would be a waste of time for both of us. I've decided to find myself another decorator.'

'Yes, I quite understand that...but it's not about the villa...'

Laura swallowed nervously, then took a deep breath and hurriedly pulled herself together. She hadn't come all this way to get tongue-tied at the crucial moment. In a clear tone, she told him,

'It's not about the villa, it's about us.'

'Us?' His eyebrows lifted. He turned round to face her. 'I wasn't aware there was such a thing as us any more.'

A fleeting wry smile touched his eyes as he said it. Laura found herself smiling a similar smile as she agreed,

'No, I don't suppose there is. But the us I was referring to was really the us that existed three years ago.'

'Ah, that us.' He seemed to sigh as he turned away again. Laura had half expected him to say that the subject no longer interested him. But he said instead, 'I thought we'd said all there was to be said about that.'

'Not quite. In fact, there's a lot that's not been said.' She paused for a moment, nervously, as though on the edge of a precipice. 'There's one point in particular that needs to be clarified.'

'And what point is that?'

'The point about my infidelity.'

There was a moment of total silence. Neither of them spoke. Even the waves seemed to have stopped lapping against the rock. Falco dropped his arms from his knees and turned to face her. 'You mean your infidelity with that antiques dealer?' he said at last.

Laura nodded. She could feel her heart pounding inside her. And suddenly, belatedly, she found herself wondering: How had he come to know the man was an antiques dealer?

But that was a digression. She summoned all her strength to keep her attention fixed on Falco's face that seemed to be swimming strangely in and out of focus.

She told him, 'Except there was no infidelity. There was never even anything close to infidelity. I did business with the man, and even that I found unpalatable.'

There was another endless silence. Then Falco spoke.

'I thought he was supposed to have been the best lover you ever had?'

No, that was you. She came close to saying it. The best and only lover I've ever had is you. But she bit the words back. To say such things was not why she had come here.

Laura took a deep breath. 'I only said that to hurt you. To hurt your pride because of the way you'd hurt me. You accused me of being unfaithful with no cause at all. You yelled and shouted at me and called me a tramp when the only scrap of so-called evidence you had was seeing me climbing into another man's car.'

Suddenly, emotionally, it was all pouring out. 'You must have *wanted* to believe it to be so easily convinced. And how could you? How could you ever have believed such a thing of me?'

Falco's eyes were narrowed. He was shaking his head. 'Oh, no,' he was saying, 'that's not the way it was. I can assure you there was a great deal more to it than that.' Then he paused as a thought seemed suddenly to strike him. He leaned towards Laura, his dark eyes narrowed. 'How did you meet that antiques dealer?' he asked.

What a peculiar question! But Laura answered it. She sensed he had a good reason for asking it.

'He phoned me up, right out of the blue. He told me he'd heard I was looking for furniture and said he was prepared to offer me a discount.'

'You'd never heard of him before?'

'Never in my life. The first time I set eyes on him was when he came to pick me up and take me personally to visit his showroom.'

Beneath his suntan Falco seemed to have grown pale. And behind the dark eyes Laura could see his brain working with a kind of tormented, desperate urgency.

She leaned towards him, suddenly impatient. 'Why are you asking all these questions? What difference does it make how I met the wretched man?'

'It matters. It matters.' He closed his eyes and shook his head. Laura could sense the pain that had taken grip of his heart. Then he sighed a sigh that shook his whole body, and leaned back against the rock, face tilted to the sky.

'That man came to me in the hotel where I was staying when I came down to London to look for you,' he continued. 'He made a hell of a scene, playing the jealous lover, telling me that I ought to go back where I'd come from, that you didn't want to see me, that you and he were in love...'

'He what?' Every muscle in Laura's body had stiffened. Her stomach was churning. She felt she might be sick.

Falco continued, his eyes still fixed on the sky, as though he could not bear to look into her face, 'That was before I'd had a chance to come and see you. The detective agency had just told me where you were living. I was more or less on my way there when he arrived, flourishing his business card and spinning his yarn. He told me he had a friend at the detective agency and that they had told him I was trying to find you.'

In a gesture filled with helpless frustration Falco dragged his fingers through his hair. 'Like a fool, I believed him. He was so damned convincing.' He let out an oath. 'But I'll bet I know who put him up to it... I'll bet I know who set the whole thing up... who gave him your phone number and hired him to come to my hotel and made sure I saw the two of you together...'

He paused to draw in a harsh, angry breath. 'I'll bet I know precisely who was at the bottom of the whole thing. I ought to have guessed it a long time ago. Who else could it possibly have been but my father?'

As Falco turned then to look at her, suddenly Laura understood, too. They'd been victims, both of them. Innocent victims of the malicious ingenuity of Oscar Roth.

'He must even have had the detective agency in his pocket.' Suddenly, it was all startlingly, sickeningly clear. 'They must have told him before they told you where I was staying, so he could set things up with the antiques dealer. Oh, God.' Laura shook her head and dropped her face in her hands. 'What a wicked, evil man your father is.'

'I know. I suppose I've always known it.' Falco had closed his eyes. His whole body was trembling. 'At first I fought against it. I tried not to believe it. It's not the sort of thing any son wants to believe about his father. But, in the end I had no choice but to face it...'

Laura raised her face then. 'And still you remained faithful. That's the thing I can't understand.'

Falco's eyes swept round to look at her. 'Faithful?' he queried. Then he smiled a wry smile and shook his head slowly. 'No, Laura,' he told her. 'My father and I went our separate ways a long time ago. We haven't even spoken to one another for years.'

'But what about the business? Roth Engineering? Surely you're still involved with that?'

'Definitely not. I want no part of it. I've had no part of it for years. These days I work full time as an art dealer.'

He paused for a moment, his eyes searching her face. Then he told her in a tone that was thick with emotion, 'I broke off all contact with my father and the business three years ago, after the débâcle with you. I didn't know then that he'd set the whole thing up, but it was enough for me to know he'd offered you money to leave me. I couldn't bear even to look at him after that.'

There was a moment's thunderous silence. How dreadfully she had misjudged him! Laura's heart was in her eyes. 'Oh, Falco, I'm so sorry!'

He reached out to take her hand. 'You've no reason to feel sorry. None of it was your fault. It was my fault, if anything. He was my father. I should have known.'

'But I lied to you, and I kept on lying! I told you I'd been unfaithful! If I hadn't done that——'

But Falco cut through her protest. 'I can understand why you said what you did.' He raised her hand to his lips and softly kissed it. 'And I can understand why you've gone on saying it. You have every right to be angry with me.'

'Yes, I was angry with you . . .' Laura paused and glanced away. Her heart was ticking like a time bomb in her chest, as she gathered her courage for her final revelation. 'But I wasn't just angry, I was also afraid.'

'Afraid?' Falco frowned. 'What could you possible be afraid of?'

Laura took a deep breath, remembering again what she had finally understood this morning at dawn. She had nothing to be afraid of. Falco was a good man. He would never try to take her daughter away from her. And he did have a right to know that Belle was his, just as Belle had a right to know her wonderful father.

Laura had wept as she had finally confronted these truths. He *was* a good man. A wonderful man. And in her heart, in spite of everything, she had never really stopped loving him.

Biting her lip now, scarcely daring to look at him, she said, her voice barely more than a whisper, 'I was afraid for Belle. Belle, my daughter——'

But that was as far as she got. Falco was leaning towards her, suddenly realising the full implications of what she'd told him.

'If that man was never your lover, then he can't be your daughter's father... So, who is her father? Was there some other man?'

'Never. There has never been any other man.'

'Then...' Falco stopped short as though he could not believe the truth that was suddenly spread out before him. He smiled like a man who had just won the lottery, yet feared that it might still be snatched away from him. 'You mean...?' He stopped short and shook his head. For the first time since Laura had known him, he was lost for words.

Laura smiled back at him and took the hands he was reaching out to her. 'I mean that you're Belle's father. You have a little girl.'

The next moment, with a cry of joy and wonder, Falco was sweeping her into his arms. 'I can't believe it. I've prayed she might be. I couldn't bear the thought of you having a child to another man.'

Then he was drawing away with a pained look to gaze at her. 'But how could you keep this a secret for so long? Even that last time we met in London... You must have known then?'

Laura shook her head wryly, 'No, I didn't. I was late, of course—my period, I mean. But I just put it down to all the emotional trauma I'd been through. It was only a couple of weeks later that I began to suspect...'

As she broke off, he caught hold of her and held her against him. 'It must have been awful for you, down in London, all alone. Oh, my love, forgive me for all these years of pain. If only I'd known...' He gazed down into her face, dark eyes filled with remorse. 'Was this what you really meant to tell me when you sent me that letter?'

'Yes.' Laura nodded.

'And I pushed you away.' He sounded as though his heart was breaking.

Laura kissed his face softly. 'Don't blame yourself. We both know the only one to blame is your father.' Then she smiled. 'Belle's only two. She has her whole life before her. And you can be a part of that life now. We can work something out.'

'Work something out?' He fixed her with a long look.

'Yes. You can visit. You can see her whenever you like.'

Still his eyes were on her. He said in a soft tone, 'I'm afraid I want a much bigger part in her life than that.'

Laura's heart turned over then. Fear poured through her. Had she been wrong, after all? Would he try to take Belle away?

Falco drew back a little, still holding her hands lightly. He said, 'I have a confession to make.'

Laura forced a tremulous smile. 'What kind of confession?' Suddenly, she was almost wishing that she had never come.

'I lied to you.' The dark eyes regarded her earnestly.

Laura swallowed drily. 'Lied? About what?'

'About how I brought you here.' He held her hands more tightly. 'You were right, it was no accident that Janine hired you. I sent her to London to do precisely that...and not to mention my name to you, on pain of death.' He smiled. 'Janine knew nothing of what was going on, nor that I had ever known you in the past...'

As he paused, Laura's heart felt tight inside her. 'And what was going on? Why did you want to hire me?' she asked.

Falco smiled. 'Partly because you're a damned good decorator...' Then his eyes once more grew serious. 'But more importantly because I wanted, finally, to get to the bottom of things. I've never been happy with the way it all ended between us. In spite of all the evidence, somehow it just didn't add up.'

He sighed. 'I've always regretted responding to your letter as I did. It caught me on a bad day. I reacted hastily. And, ever since, I've wondered what it was you wanted to say to me. I decided it was time I finally found out. And that was why I hatched my devious little plot to bring you here.'

Laura could not move. Transfixed, she gazed into his face and listened in silence as he continued, 'But you made it so hard for me.' A frown touched his brow. 'I provoked you and pushed you and tried every way I knew how to get you to tell me what you were holding back. At times you forced me to behave like a monster.' He smiled a wry smile. 'But I was utterly determined. And do you want to know why?'

Her heart pounding, Laura nodded. She was incapable of speech.

'I was determined because I knew I'd never rest till I succeeded. As hard as I've tried, I've never managed to forget you.' He paused, his eyes seeming to pour into hers. 'You're the only woman I've ever truly loved. The only woman I'll love until the day I die.'

Laura's heart had suddenly stopped inside her. These were words she'd dreamed of hearing, though she'd never dared admit it. Her face alight with joy, she looked into his eyes, as he continued, 'That's why, I'm afraid, I must insist on playing a somewhat larger part in our daughter's life than you suggested.' As Laura held her breath, he kissed her softly. 'What I'm afraid I must insist on is that you marry me and allow me to be a proper father to our daughter.'

Laura looked back at him, her heart twisting inside her with happiness. 'I'll marry you,' she told him. 'I love you, Falco. And I know you'll be a wonderful father.'

A moment later they were falling into one another's arms, clinging to one another, exchanging fierce kisses, their hearts soaring to the sky, the past at last behind them, knowing that from now until forever nothing and no one could ever separate them again.

'There's just one thing you still haven't explained.' Falco turned his head to look at her. 'That flat in St John's Wood. How did you happen to be there?'

They were down on the stretch of beach just beyond the villa gardens, lying together on the warm pale sand while a blood-red sun dipped slowly over the horizon.

Laura smiled. 'I came to be in that flat by a simple piece of good fortune.'

She reached out and touched his face, then with loving fingers smoothed the dark silky hair from his forehead. In the space of a few hours the whole world has changed, she was thinking. For it was only a few hours since their encounter on the rock, though the moments before that seemed to belong now to another lifetime.

They had returned to the villa in Falco's car, with Laura's bicycle stowed safely in the boot. And throughout the journey not a word had passed between them. There had been no need for words. A halo of happiness surrounded them, as they had exchanged looks and smiles, two people suddenly one, Falco's hand releasing hers only when he had to change gear.

Then still without a word, knowing it was what they both wanted, they had gone straight to Falco's bedroom and locked the door behind them. And there, with all the pent-up love and passion that had been denied expression for too many years, they had made love to one another, hungrily, joyfully, two people suddenly released from a nightmare into a dream.

For a long time afterwards they had lain together peacefully, limbs entwined in the big double bed, talking, not talking, kissing, caressing, bound by the bonds of love that had never been broken.

And now, after a light supper, they had drifted down to the beach to lie together and watch the sunset.

Falco caught her hand and kissed it. 'What kind of good fortune?' he asked her. 'Go on, explain. How did you come to be in that house?'

As he drew her into his arms, Laura rested her chin on his shoulder, looked into his eyes and told him her story.

'You probably don't remember Mrs Hamilton? An old lady. A neighbour of my parents.'

'Of course I remember her. At least, I remember you speaking about her. You used to run errands for her and things like that.'

'Fancy you remembering!' Laura poked him playfully.

'I remember everything about us.' He kissed her nose. 'Now kindly continue with your story.'

'Well, Mrs Hamilton had a sister, a wealthy widow who lived in London, in that very flat in St John's Wood. I never knew about the sister until she died. It happened while you were on that business trip in Brussels...' Her voice faltered for an instant. She felt a coldness inside her. Then, as Falco held her close for a moment, she carried on,

'The sister left the flat and all her money to Mrs Hamilton, and, really as a favour to me, because she knew about my ambition to become a decorator, Mrs Hamilton asked me to do up the flat...'

She took a deep breath. This part was painful. 'It all happened around the time that your father issued his ultimatum and demanded that I get out of town. It seemed the perfect opportunity and I had nowhere else to go, so I said yes.' She smiled. 'And that was what I was doing there.'

Falco stroked her hair softly. 'Such a simple explanation.' His voice was filled with regret. 'If only I'd known.'

'How could you have known? I didn't tell you and I'd sworn my parents to total secrecy. If they'd told you where I was or anything at all about my circumstances, it would only have rebounded on my father.'

Laura sighed. 'Sometimes I think it was more of a curse than a lucky break being given that job in that St John's Wood flat. If you'd found me living in some bedsitter in Ladbroke Grove, you wouldn't have believed I'd taken the money and we might never have been parted.'

'I think you underestimate my father.' Falco shook his head, his expression sombre. 'He would have been forced to invent a whole different scenario, but he would have thought of something that was guaranteed to drive us apart.

'But let's not talk about my father.' He tilted her chin and kissed her. 'Tell me about the St John's Wood flat. That, I take it, was what launched your career?'

Laura nodded, then confessed, 'I lied to you about that. I told you I got my first commission simply by telling the other residents that I was an interior designer.' She pulled an apologetic face. 'The real truth is that when the woman in the next apartment saw the job I'd done on Mrs Hamilton's flat, she instantly demanded that I do hers too. And from there it simply snowballed. All this woman's friends suddenly wanted me to do up their houses.'

Falco laughed and kissed her. 'Next stop Buckingham Palace!' There was pride in his voice. He hugged her warmly. 'I wouldn't be surprised if one day that really happens.'

It was wonderful to feel his arms around her. Laura buried her face against his neck and kissed him. She had forgotten how it felt to be this happy.

Then she looked up into his eyes. 'But, first things first. First, I have a small commission on Alba to complete. That is,' she added, smiling, 'unless you're still determined to find yourself another decorator?'

'No, I've gone off that idea.' Falco was laughing. Then his expression grew more sober. 'You're going to do it—with your husband and your little daughter here to keep an eye on you and make sure you do the best possible job.'

As they gazed at one another, the sun suddenly disappeared, only a streak of bright crimson still lighting the horizon.

Neither of them noticed. They were lost in one another.

'But, before all that...' Falco suddenly bent to kiss her '...I want to take you back to the villa and make love to you all over again. We still have a lot of catching up to do.'

'Let's go, then. What are we waiting for?' Laura was smiling happily, as Falco rose to his feet, drawing her with him. She slipped her arms around his neck, stood on tiptoe and kissed the tiny mole in the corner of his eye.

And as she clung to him, she could have wept for the happiness that possessed her and for the happiness she could see shining back at her from Falco's eyes.

As the stars came out and the pale moon shone, like an omen of all the joy and contentment that lay before them, she leaned against him as he slipped his arm around her shoulders and led her across the still-warm sand to the villa and the first of many, many nights of love.

Next Month's Romances

Each month you can choose from a wide variety of romance with Mills & Boon. Below are the new titles to look out for next month, why not ask either Mills & Boon Reader Service or your Newsagent to reserve you a copy of the titles you want to buy — just tick the titles you would like and either post to Reader Service or take it to any Newsagent and ask them to order your books.

Please save me the following titles:	Please tick	√
HIGH RISK	Emma Darcy	
PAGAN SURRENDER	Robyn Donald	
YESTERDAY'S ECHOES	Penny Jordan	
PASSIONATE CAPTIVITY	Patricia Wilson	
LOVE OF MY HEART	Emma Richmond	
RELATIVE VALUES	Jessica Steele	
TRAIL OF LOVE	Amanda Browning	
THE SPANISH CONNECTION	Kay Thorpe	
SOMETHING MISSING	Kate Walker	
SOUTHERN PASSIONS	Sara Wood	
FORGIVE AND FORGET	Elizabeth Barnes	
YESTERDAY'S DREAMS	Margaret Mayo	
STORM OF PASSION	Jenny Cartwright	
MIDNIGHT STRANGER	Jessica Marchant	
WILDER'S WILDERNESS	Miriam Macgregor	
ONLY TWO CAN SHARE	Annabel Murray	

If you would like to order these books in addition to your regular subscription from Mills & Boon Reader Service please send £1.80 per title to: Mills & Boon Reader Service, Freepost, P.O. Box 236, Croydon, Surrey, CR9 9EL, quote your Subscriber No:................................... (If applicable) and complete the name and address details below. Alternatively, these books are available from many local Newsagents including W.H.Smith, J.Menzies, Martins and other paperback stockists from 14th May 1993.

Name:...

Address:...

....Post Code:...........................

To Retailer: If you would like to stock M&B books please contact your regular book/magazine wholesaler for details.

You may be mailed with offers from other reputable companies as a result of this application. If you would rather not take advantage of these opportunities please tick box ☐

An irresistible offer from Mills & Boon

Here's a personal invitation from Mills & Boon Reader Service, to become a regular reader of Romances. To welcome you, we'd like you to have 4 books, a CUDDLY TEDDY and a special MYSTERY GIFT absolutely FREE.

Then you could look forward each month to receiving 6 brand new Romances, delivered to your door, postage and packing free! Plus our free Newsletter featuring author news, competitions, special offers and much more.

This invitation comes with no strings attached. You may cancel or suspend your subscription at any time, and still keep your free books and gifts.

It's so easy. Send no money now. Simply fill in the coupon below and post it to -
Reader Service, FREEPOST, PO Box 236, Croydon, Surrey CR9 9EL.

NO STAMP REQUIRED

Free Books Coupon

Yes! Please rush me 4 free Romances and 2 free gifts! Please also reserve me a Reader Service subscription. If I decide to subscribe I can look forward to receiving 6 brand new Romances each month for just £10.20, postage and packing free. If I choose not to subscribe I shall write to you within 10 days - I can keep the books and gifts whatever I decide. I may cancel or suspend my subscription at any time. I am over 18 years of age.

Ms/Mrs/Miss/Mr_____ EP31R

Address _____

_____

Postcode_____ Signature _____